THE TALE OF
TOM TIDDLER

www.randomhousechildrens.co.uk

Also by Eleanor Farjeon:

Martin Pippin in the Daisy Field
Martin Pippin in the Apple Orchard

The Glass Slipper
Perkin the Pedlar
Jim at the Corner
Kaleidoscope
The Old Nurse's Stocking-Basket
The New Book of Days
Nursery Rhymes of London Town

THE TALE OF
TOM TIDDLER

Eleanor Farjeon

RED FOX CLASSICS

THE TALE OF TOM TIDDLER
A RED FOX CLASSICS BOOK 978 1 849 41936 9

First published in Great Britain by W. Collins Sons & Co Ltd
This edition published 2013
First published 1929

1 3 5 7 9 10 8 6 4 2

The Random House Group Limited supports The Forest Stewardship
Council® (FSC®), the leading international forest-certification organisation.
Our books carrying the FSC label are printed on FSC®-certified paper.
FSC is the only forest-certification scheme supported by the leading
environmental organisations, including Greenpeace. Our
paper procurement policy can be found at
www.randomhouse.co.uk/environment

Set in Bembo 12/17pt by Falcon Oast Graphic Art Ltd.

Random House Children's Publishers UK,
61–63 Uxbridge Road, London W5 5SA

www.randomhousechildrens.co.uk
www.totallyrandombooks.co.uk
www.randomhouse.co.uk

Addresses for companies within The Random House Group Limited can be
found at: www.randomhouse.co.uk/offices.htm

THE RANDOM HOUSE GROUP Limited Reg. No. 954009

A CIP catalogue record for this book is available from the British Library.

Printed and bound in Great Britain by Clays Ltd, St Ives plc

1

GOLD AND SILVER

TOM TIDDLER WAS born in a hollow oak, in a buttercup-and-daisy field. The day before he was born his father picked up a purse with ten pounds in it, and bought the field because he liked it, and had nowhere to go. After Mr. Tiddler bought the field he and Mrs. Tiddler always had somewhere to go, and they never went anywhere else.

Why should they? There was everything in the field that the heart could desire. In the middle of it was the hollow oak in which Tom Tiddler was born. It was an enormous tree, and had a great cave in its trunk; each of its big boughs was a room in itself, broad enough to dance on, or curl up and go to sleep on; and each little bough was a stairway leading to the next landing. On one of the boughs lived a Brown Owl called Simon. The oak-tree was Tom Tiddler's house.

Besides the oak-tree, the field had a pool in it, as round as a soup-plate, but seventy times as wide and forty times as deep. The pool was Tom Tiddler's bath.

Besides the pool, the field had a hedge all round it of nut-trees and blackberry bushes, elder-bushes and wild raspberry canes; so that he had fruit to eat and nuts to crack, and elderberry wine to sip. The hedge was Tom Tiddler's larder.

Besides the hedge, the field had mushrooms in it, for the sheep used to stray in to crop the sweet grass, and where there are sheep there are mushrooms. The Tiddlers liked nothing better than fried mushrooms except stewed ones, and nothing better than stewed mushrooms except fried ones. The mushrooms were Tom Tiddler's treat.

Besides the mushrooms, the field had wool in it, for the lambs left tufts of their fleece on the brambles; and Mrs. Tiddler picked it off again, and spun it on her spindle. The wool was Tom Tiddler's clothes.

Besides the lamb's-wool to wear, there was some one to play with, whenever Jerry the Goat from the Common came gambolling through the hedge to munch whatever he could find on the other side. The goat was Tom Tiddler's company.

And besides the goat, the lamb's-wool, the mushrooms, the hedges, the pool and the oak-tree, the field had buttercups and daisies in it spring, summer, and autumn. The buttercups and daisies were Tom Tiddler's treasure.

When Tom Tiddler was ten years old, he woke up one morning, and his Father and Mother weren't there.

'That's funny!' said Tom Tiddler.

He hunted high and he hunted low, but never a sign of them did he see.

'Dear me!' said Tom Tiddler.

He called up and he called down, but never a sound of them did he hear.

'Oh well!' said Tom Tiddler.

He picked the mushrooms that had grown up in the night, and fried them in his Mother's pan for breakfast. He was a handy boy, and could do most of the things his Father and Mother did. He could spin his clothes of lamb's-wool, and put them on when they were made. He could lay a fire of sticks, and warm his hands at it when it was lit. And he could cook his breakfast and supper, and eat them when they were ready.

So he did not find himself at a loss when his Father and Mother never came back. But after a while he began to miss them badly, because he had nobody to talk to but Himself. Every morning he went first thing to look at Himself in the pool, and there he saw Himself looking up with his round blue eyes, his fuzzy red head, and his turned-up nose with the freckle on the tip.

'Good-morning!' said Tom to Himself.

'Good-morning!' said Himself to Tom.

3

'And what sort of night did you have?' asked Tom Tiddler.

'And what sort of night did *you* have?' asked Himself.

'Last night I dreamed about a mushroom three yards round,' said Tom.

'Last night *I* dreamed about a mushroom three yards round,' said Himself.

'I knew that already, silly!' said Tom Tiddler, rather cross.

'Silly!' said Himself, just as cross as Tom was.

Then Tom wouldn't speak to Himself for an hour or more.

The funny thing was, that though Jerry and the sheep came into his field, it never occurred to Tom to go out of it. He thought that his four hedges were the end of everything, and where Jerry came from he never inquired.

But one night he woke up suddenly, and peeping out of the oak-tree saw a child in his field picking his buttercups and daisies.

'What are you doing?' cried Tom.

The child jumped like a hare, and ran away as though the farmer was after her.

'Come back!' called Tom.

'I won't!' called the child.

'What are you doing on *my* ground?' called Tom again.

'Picking up gold and silver!' called the child.

'Who are you?' called Tom.

'Jinny Jones,' called the child. 'Who are *you*?'

'Tom Tiddler,' called Tom. 'Come here!'

'I *won't*!' called Jinny Jones. 'You can't catch *me*, Tom Tiddler!'

And she was gone.

'Oh well,' said Tom, and went to sleep again.

But the next night he kept watch, and presently in she came, with Mary Brown and Betty Green. For Jinny Jones had told them she'd found a field where grew such silver daisies and such golden buttercups as never were.

As soon as he saw them, Tom jumped out of his tree and tried to catch them. Then Mary Brown cried,

'Here we come to Tom Tiddler's Ground—'

'Picking up Gold and Silver!' added Betty Green.

And Jinny Jones laughed, 'You can't catch *me*!' And they ran away with their aprons full of flowers.

After this, it became a game with the little girls all round the countryside to venture into Tom Tiddler's ground at night to pick his buttercups and daisies when he wasn't looking. And though he always tried to catch one, in the end they managed to slip outside, where Tom never went because he didn't know it was there.

Still, he was no longer lonely as he used to be before the children came picking up Gold and Silver.

2

HOW TOM TIDDLER CAUGHT SIMON THE OWL

ONE NIGHT JINNY Jones didn't come as usual. Tom asked the other children, 'Where's Jinny Jones?'

'We don't know,' said the children. 'She wasn't in school to-day.'

The next night another child was missing, and Tom Tiddler asked, 'Where are Jinny Jones and Mary Brown?'

'We don't know,' said the children. 'They weren't at lessons this morning.'

The next night still another child was wanting, and Tom asked, 'Where are Jinny Jones and Mary Brown and Betty Green?'

'We don't know,' said the children. 'They missed the School-Treat this afternoon.'

This went on night after night, and one night no children came at all. Then Tom Tiddler sat down in the middle of his gold and silver and felt very badly.

While he was sitting there he heard a long-drawn call float over the field: 'Whoo–oo! Tu-whit tu-whoo–oo!'

It was Simon the Owl flying low in search of mice. At the same moment came a long-drawn bleat from the hedge: 'Meehmeh-meehh-hh!' It was Jerry the Goat poking through in search of grass.

When they saw Tom Tiddler feeling so badly, they stopped and considered him.

'What's the matter with him?' asked Jerry, who knew nothing.

'He's missing Jinny Jones,' answered Simon, who knew everything.

This was the first time Tom had heard them talk.

'What has happened to Jinny Jones?' asked Jerry.

'She has been carried off by Gogmagog the Giant,' said Simon, 'with all the other little girls.'

'How do you know?' asked Jerry.

'I know everything,' said Simon.

'Oh, you do, do you?' cried Tom Tiddler, jumping up. 'Then you know where Gogmagog has taken them to.'

'Yes,' said Simon, 'I know that too.'

'Tell me where,' said Tom.

'Ah, but that,' said Simon, 'would be telling.'

'Of course it would,' said Tom. 'Why shouldn't it be? What's the good of knowing if you don't tell?'

'If I told all I know,' said Simon, 'there'd be nothing left to find out.'

'You *shall* tell me!' shouted Tom, and made a grab at him, but Simon flew up to the top of the oak-tree, far out of reach. Then Tom made a grab at Jerry, but Jerry put down his head, bowled him over, and trotted off down the field.

So Tom threw himself on the ground again, feeling more badly than ever. In fact, for the first time in his life he began to cry, with his face in the buttercups and daisies. They stood all up around his ears, and as his tears flowed he could hear them whispering together.

'Dear me!' said a daisy, 'how heavy the dew is tonight.'

'That's not dew, that's Tom Tiddler crying,' said a buttercup.

'What's he crying for?'

'For Jinny Jones.'

'What's the matter with her?'

'She has been stolen away.'

'Why doesn't he go and find her?'

'Because he can't till he catches Simon, and there's only one way to do that.'

'What is it?'

'By starving Jerry of food, till he comes to be fed. Where Jerry is, there Simon will be.'

'Why?' asked the daisy.

'Bed-time!' said the buttercup. 'Shut your eyes and go to sleep.'

Then there was no more talking.

But Tom had heard all he wanted to. He lost no time in setting to work. First he stopped up the gap in the hedge, so that Jerry couldn't get out. Next he pulled up all the grass in the field, stripped all the leaves and berries from the bushes, and stuffed them into the pool. Not a blade or a leaf was left for Jerry to crop, and when he came to the pool Tom drove him away with a stick. At the end of three days Jerry came to Tom and said, 'Give me my dinner, and I'll follow you wherever you go.'

'Very well,' said Tom, and at once undid the gap in the hedge, while Jerry stood by as meek as a lamb.

Seeing this, Simon flew down from his tree, and perching on Tom's shoulder said, 'So you've got Jerry, have you?'

'Yes. I starved him,' said Tom.

'How clever!' said Simon. 'You don't need me, I see.'

'But I starved myself too,' added Tom.

'How stupid!' said Simon. 'I see you need me badly.'

That was how Tom Tiddler got hold of Jerry the Goat and Simon the Owl when he set forth to find Jinny Jones.

3

TOM TIDDLER MEETS ARRY

IT WAS A great surprise to Tom Tiddler to find that the four hedges round his field were not the four walls round everywhere, and that the world was a bigger place than he supposed it was.

He stood with his back to the hedge and saw a road in front of him, a common to the right of him, and a wood to the left of him.

'Dear me!' said Tom Tiddler, scratching his head, 'whichever way shall I go to find Jinny Jones?'

'Go straight on!' hooted Simon.

'Go sideways!' bleated Jerry.

'I can't do both,' said Tom.

'Do as you like,' said Simon, 'but Jerry is only thinking of the grass on the common, and he doesn't care a thistle for Jinny Jones. If you're sensible you'll go straight on and ask a lift of the very first man you meet.'

So Tom walked straight on, while Simon flew before him and Jerry capered after him.

He hadn't walked a mile before he heard a

jingle on the road, and along came a Coster's cart drawn by a little grey Moke with bells on her harness.

The Coster was sitting on a heap of fresh cabbages, and he had on his best suit, covered with pearlies. His Moke was as gay as he was, for she had a brass star on her forehead, a red tassel on her tail, and on her pointed ears were cases of scarlet leather. Tom recognised them at once as Jinny Jones's little scarlet slippers. So he stood in the middle of the road and shouted—

'Stop!'

The Coster pulled up and said, 'What's the matter, matey?'

'I know *your* name,' said Tom very fiercely.

'Who sez you didn't?' asked the Coster.

'You're Gogmagog the Giant!' said Tom. 'Where's Jinny Jones?'

'Bless yer buttons!' said the Coster; 'me name is Arry, and Gogmagog could put me and my Moke-and-cart into his waistcoat pocket. And as for Jinny Jones, I never heard of her.'

'Those are her slippers,' said Tom, pointing to the little Moke's ears.

'Who sez they ain't?' asked the Coster. 'I picked 'em up last week on my way to Covent Garden.'

'Where did you find them?' asked Tom.

'One just outside London Town, and t'other just inside,' said Arry.

'Will you give me a lift to London Town?' asked Tom.

'Op up!' said Arry.

Tom hopped up, and sat himself down on the fattest cabbage he could find. Off trotted the moke, and after them trotted Jerry. Simon had sunk his head in his neck-feathers, and gone to sleep on Tom's shoulder. But Jerry kept wide awake, and snatched a cabbage off the back of the cart whenever he got the chance.

While they trotted along, Arry told Tom that London Town would suit him down to the ground. 'For,' said Arry, ''tis paved with gold and silver, enough to fill yer pockets a hundred times over every day for a year. Many a boy goes there to seek his fortune. Look at me! I went there without a pair o' shoes to my feet, and now I've got pearlies and a cabbage-patch of my own. But I ought to warn yer that the town is full of dangers.'

'What sort of dangers?' asked Tom.

'This Gogmagog for one. He steals little girls wherever he finds 'em, and makes them his servants. They have to fan the flies off him when he goes to sleep. He needs a lot of 'em, because there's such a lot of *him*. The one that fans his nose and the one that fans his toes are so far apart that they can't even see each other.

But there's many a difficulty to overcome besides Gogmagog. Such as the Moor, and the Spaniards, and Bugsby, to mention just a few. You'll be lucky if you come out with a whole skin. Now, will yer turn back, or will yer go on?'

'Turn back!' bleated Jerry.

'Go on!' muttered Simon.

'I'll go on,' said Tom Tiddler, 'and trust to luck.'

'That's yer sort!' said Arry. 'And there's one o' the gates o' London Town in sight. Bless my buttons if that goat of yours hasn't gobbled arf my cabbages!'

Arry pulled up so suddenly to aim a blow at Jerry, that Tom toppled out of the cart backwards, and all the cabbages rolled atop of him. Feeling her load lightened, the little Moke galloped off like a racehorse, and pull as he might Arry couldn't stop her. In another moment he and his Moke and his cart had disappeared through the gate, and Tom was left sitting among the cabbages.

'That,' said Simon, waking up, very ruffled, 'is what comes of being greedy.'

'And a very good thing too!' said Jerry, and began to munch cabbages for all he was worth.

Tom Tiddler was perfectly contented too, for here he was at London Town, and somewhere inside was Jinny Jones.

So Simon had to be huffy all by himself.

4

THE MOOR'S GATE

WHEN TOM SAW London in front of him, he went up to the gate and peeped in. It was a beautiful fretwork gate of gold and red and blue and green. On the wall on one side hung a great iron file on a nail. Against the opposite wall grew a date-palm-tree, with the Gatehouse under it. The Gatehouse was painted pink, and had a glittering golden dome, through the door of which issued a cloud of delicious-smelling steam.

Jerry sniffed the air and bleated, 'Coffee!'

'Coffee!' echoed Tom. 'How good it smells!'

'Shut your noses,' hooted Simon, 'and go straight on.'

'Not me!' said Jerry obstinately. 'I shall go in and have some.'

'Yes, where's the harm?' asked Tom.

'Find out!' snapped Simon, 'and don't blame me.'

'Stuff and nonsense!' said Jerry. He blundered through the golden door, Tom after him.

There, standing over a golden brazier watching a

golden coffee-pot, stood a Moor seven feet high, and as brown as a coffee-bean. He wore a pure white robe, a red silk headcloth, a red silk sash fringed with gold, and golden shoes turned up at the points. On his left leg was an anklet attached to a heavy chain, the other end of which was fixed to a ring in the wall.

On seeing Tom, he shot out a great brown hand and gripped him, thundering,

'How dare you enter the Moor's Gate without knocking, boy? Have you the Freedom of the City?'

'No,' said Tom, who didn't know what he was talking about. 'Have you?'

'Look at my chain and ask!' said the Moor bitterly. 'I have no freedom of any sort. Mocha-el-Mocha is my name. Many years ago I sailed here in a golden galley from Spain, with three rascally Spaniards for my servants. I had already conquered Spain, and now I meant to conquer London Town. But while I slept the rascally Spaniards betrayed me to King Lud, for a bit of land. King Lud made me the keeper of this gate, and chained me as you see, saying that not till I could compel someone to take my place should I go free. To torment me he hung up that great file on the wall just out of my reach. My chain allows me only to touch it with the tip of my middle finger. But now your Owl shall bring it to me, and you shall file through my chain.

Then I will chain you in my place, roast your goat for my supper, and go back to my own country.'

'That won't be very pleasant for me,' grumbled Jerry.

'It isn't supposed to be,' said Mocha–el–Mocha, with a grim laugh.

'May I have a drink of coffee first?' asked Jerry.

'When I am filed free,' said the Moor, 'and your young master is chained up. Not before.'

'Do be quick, Simon,' said Jerry, 'and fetch the file.'

'The quicker he is,' said the Moor, 'the quicker you'll roast.'

'And the quicker I'll get my coffee,' said Jerry. 'What comes first comes first.'

Tom looked at Simon, and Simon looked at Tom, and brought the file in his beak. Then, while Mocha–el–Mocha held Tom fast with his right hand and drank coffee with his left, Tom began to file away the chain. All the while he was thinking: 'If only I dared ask Simon what to do!'

Presently he dropped the file and put his hand to his head, as though in agony.

'Why do you stop?' thundered the Moor.

'Sir,' said Tom, 'the squeaking of the file hurts my ears. If I do not cover them up I shall faint. Perhaps you will permit my Owl to sit on my shoulder and cover my ears with his wings.'

'As you please,' said the Moor.

Simon at once perched on Tom's shoulder, and spread his big soft wings round Tom's head. Then he tucked his own head under his wing and whispered in Tom's ear,

'Just see what danger you are in, Tom Tiddler, through not following my advice to begin with. The only remedy against Moors is to slip a date-stone into their left shoe, which, as everybody knows, gives them a severe cramp for exactly half a minute.'

Tom went on filing for a moment or two, and then, dropping the file, put his hand to his stomach as though in acute distress.

'What is it now?' thundered the Moor.

'Sir,' said Tom, 'I have had nothing to eat since yesterday morning, and I feel so hungry that I fear I shall faint. Perhaps you will permit my Owl to fetch me a date from your palm-tree outside.'

'As you please,' said the Moor.

Simon instantly flew out, and returned with a date, which Tom ate with great enjoyment, concealing the stone in his hand. As soon as he picked up the file and had his fingers on the Moor's left ankle, he pushed the stone well into Mocha-el-Mocha's golden slipper.

The Moor set up a roar that shook the walls of

London, and letting go of Tom's shoulder he grasped his left toe in his hand to ease the pain.

'Quick!' cried Tom, 'we have only half a minute!'

He dashed out of the Gatehouse, followed by Simon and Jerry, while the Moor, roaring louder with anger than he had roared with pain, dashed after them. But they were already out of reach, and Tom was hanging up the file on its nail again.

'You see now,' said Simon, 'where stupidity leads you. If you hadn't gone in so quick, you wouldn't have run the risk of being chained to the wall, and roasted at the fire.'

'Yes,' grumbled Jerry, 'and if we hadn't come out so quick we would have had some coffee.'

5

THE KING'S CHERRY-SELLER

AFTER HE HAD escaped from the Moor at the Gate, Tom Tiddler said to Simon, 'What shall we do next to find Gogmagog?'

'Have breakfast,' said Simon.

'Bother!' said Tom. 'That's wasting time.'

'Not at all,' said Simon. 'It's a very bad thing to meet a giant on an empty stomach.'

'I quite agree with you,' said Jerry, who could always eat anything anywhere at any time.

'Oh, well!' said Tom. Having lived in a field all his life, he didn't know there was anything else to have for breakfast except nuts and blackberries; so he asked the first man he saw where he could find some.

'There are plenty in Covent Garden,' said the man, and told him the way there.

In Covent Garden a great bustle was going on. There were stalls and stalls piled up with apples and carrots and peaches and onions, and fruit and vegetables of all sorts; and carts and carts kept rolling in with more. Men were shouting, women were buying, boys were carrying baskets, and berries and peas were rolling in the gutters, where children and pigeons picked them up.

In the midst of this confusion Tom saw a big fat man sitting by his stall weeping bitterly. On his stall was written:

CHERRIES

in large red and black letters, but the stall itself was as bare as a bald man's head.

'Why are you crying?' asked Tom Tiddler. 'And why does your stall say Cherries, and have none?'

'Ah, there you've hit it!' said the Cherry-Seller, mopping his fat cheeks with a handkerchief. 'I'm crying just because there are no cherries on my stall, and haven't been this month.'

'You ought to sell something else, then,' said Tom. 'There are lots of things besides cherries to put on a stall.' And he waved his hand to the heaps of pears and potatoes and grapes and cauliflowers that were being crowded on other stalls till they toppled over.

'Talk of what you know!' sobbed the big fat man. 'A Cherry-Seller I was born, and a Cherry-Seller I'll die. I am Cherry-Seller to King Lud of London, and not one cherry have I been able to sell him this season, though he sends his Cook for them every day. And every day he gets crosser and crosser because he has to go without. Hark! there's the King's Cook coming now!'

As he spoke a trumpet sounded, and a way was cleared through the cabbages and tomatoes down which marched the King's Cook, followed by his twelve Kitchen-maids. When he reached the Cherry-Seller's stall the Cook said in a very loud voice,

'What's the price of Cherries to-day?'

'Sixpence a pound,' said the Cherry-Seller.

'Then I'll have ten pounds,' said the Cook, pulling out five shillings.

'You can't have ten pounds,' said the Cherry-Seller. 'You can't have one pound. You can't have half a pound.'

Then the Cook said in a very small voice,

'Oh dear, oh dear! don't tell me there are still no cherries to be had!'

'But I *do* tell you!' said the King's Cherry-Seller, and he shook in his shoes. 'Sixpence a pound is the market-price of cherries, but not one cherry has come to market.'

Then the King's Cook shook in *his* shoes, and so did the twelve Kitchen-maids, and the Cook said, 'However shall I dare go back and tell King Lud? His crossness is getting past belief. When I told him yesterday, he was so cross that he tore his purple robe in two and threw his sceptre into the Thames. What he'll do to-day who can say?'

'But why aren't there any cherries?' asked Tom Tiddler.

'Why?' said the Cherry-Seller. 'Because all the cherries grow in the Cherry-Gardens, that's why!'

'And,' said the Cook, 'Gogmagog the Giant has gone to live there, that's why!'

'Moreover,' said the Cherry-Seller, 'he has taken all the little girls in England to pick the cherries for him, and he eats up one tree a day.'

'Because,' said the Cook, 'there are only two things Gogmagog likes to eat, cherries and little girls.'

'So,' said the Cherry-Seller, 'as long as the cherries last, the little girls are safe.'

'But,' said the Cook, 'when he has eaten the cherries he'll eat the little girls.'

'And meanwhile,' said the Cherry-Seller, 'there are no cherries at all for King Lud!'

'Who,' said the Cook, 'grows crosser and crosser and crosser, and will soon be the death of us. And *that's* why!'

Then both the Cook and the Cherry-Seller shook in their shoes again and burst into tears; and so did the twelve Kitchen-maids. But Tom Tiddler clapped his hands and shouted, 'Hurrah!'

'There's nothing to hurrah about,' said the Cherry-Seller.

'Yes, there is!' cried Tom. 'For now I know where Gogmagog is, and I can go and rescue Jinny Jones.'

He set off at a run, but suddenly stopped and said to Simon, 'I know where Gogmagog is, but where are the Cherry Gardens?'

'Over the river from Wapping Old Stairs,' said Simon.

'Come along!' shouted Tom, and began to run again; while Jerry asked,

'What about breakfast?'

'Never mind breakfast!' cried Tom, and Jerry had to gambol after him, grumbling,

'Never mind breakfast indeed! As though I did mind breakfast! What I mind is no breakfast! I never mind *breakfast*!'

But Tom paid no heed to him, and did not stop running till he reached Wapping Old Stairs.

6

BUGSBY

WHEN TOM TIDDLER reached Wapping he found that there was no bridge over the river and no boat to carry him across. There were only the Old Stairs going down to the green water that slapped and slopped against them. On the other side of the river Tom could see the Cherry Gardens, all green with leaves and rosy-red with fruit. He sat down on the top Stair, and looked and looked with all his eyes for Jinny Jones and the little girls, but saw no sign of them, or of Gogmagog.

'What shall I do?' said Tom. 'The river is wide, the water is deep and I can't swim.'

'Jump,' said Jerry.

'Don't be silly,' said Tom.

'Ask Bugsby,' said Simon.

'Who's he?' said Tom.

'He's the only person who can help you over the water. He lives in the river-bed, and has arms half a mile long. His reach stretches further even than Gogmagog's. But be sure to wait till you can get on the right side of him, which will be when the tide turns at ten o'clock. Then he will do whatever you ask him to. If by mistake you get on the wrong side of him, he will make himself very unpleasant.'

Tom went down on the bottom Stair to wait till ten o'clock. There were some stones lying on the Stairs, so he began to skip them on the water to while away the time. There is no better way of whiling time away than skipping stones, and Tom was very good at it. He wanted to make one hop right across from Wapping to the Cherry Gardens. Presently he found a splendid big flat stone.

'Now for a champion skip,' said Tom, and shot it on to the water. But he threw it badly, and after two or three hops it dropped with a splash into the water.

A moment later the water began to rise and fall as though there were an earthquake in the river-bed. Then two long thin arms with long thin hands came up and waved in the air. They were followed by a long thin head with a long thin nose; but the end of the nose, which should have been pointed, was perfectly flat. The head opened its long thin lips and snarled,

'Who threw that stone?'

'I did,' said Tom. 'It went wrong.'

'It went on my nose!' snarled the long thin man. 'Just

see what you have done to it! A moment ago my nose was as sharp as a pin, and now it's as flat as a penny. How am I going to spear fish for my dinner?'

'I don't know,' said Tom. 'I suppose you are Bugsby.'

'I'll Bugsby you!' snarled the long thin man, and stretched out one long thin hand towards the Stairs.

'I'm sorry about the stone. It was a pure accident,' said Tom; 'and I don't think I want to be Bugsbied.'

'Bugsbied you'll be, if you want to or not!' snarled Bugsby, and he stretched out the other long thin hand.

Tom saw plainly that he had got on the wrong side of Bugsby, and that there would be no getting out of the reach of a person with a reach of half a mile.

'Oh, Simon,' he whispered, 'what shall I do?'

'Try to put him off for two minutes,' whispered Simon, who had been watching the river very attentively.

So just as Bugsby was about to grab him, Tom clapped his hand on a wooden post that was driven into the water, and cried, 'Touchwood! Before you Bugsby me, give me two minutes.'

'What for?' snarled Bugsby.

'To say my Seven Times Table in,' said Tom desperately. 'I haven't said it this morning.'

'Say away then,' snarled Bugsby, 'and much good may it do you!'

Tom began, very slowly: 'Seven times one is seven, and seven times two is eight, and seven times three is nine—' because he had never been to school and knew no better. Just as he reached 'Seven times twelve is eighteen,' the clock struck ten, and Bugsby's long thin hand grabbed Tom round the middle. At the same moment the tide turned, and the river began to run the other way.

Instantly Bugsby's snarls turned into smiles.

'What can I do for you?' smiled Bugsby.

Tom now saw that he was on the right side of Bugsby, and said, 'I want to be put across the river, please.'

'And so you shall be,' smiled Bugsby; and picking Tom up with one hand and Jerry with the other, he set them down on the opposite bank, while Simon flew over by himself.

'Thank you,' said Tom. 'I'm sorry about your nose.'

'It was a pure accident,' smiled Bugsby.

'Wait a bit,' said Tom. He caught hold of Jerry's left horn, and sawed off the tip with his penknife. Jerry protested, but he had to put up with it.

'There!' said Tom. 'There's a new tip for your nose. It's quite sharp, and will spear fish beautifully.'

'I'll go at once and stick it on with fish–glue,' smiled Bugsby.

He dived out of sight, and left Tom looking through the gate into the Cherry Gardens.

7

THE BAYS' WATER

IT WAS A green lattice gate set in a high brick wall. It was locked with a padlock, and the wall had no foothold for climbing. Tom shook the gate till it rattled again, but all to no purpose. Then he pressed his face against it, and called,

'Jinny Jones! Mary Brown! Betty Green! Jinny! Jinny Jones!'

Soon he heard a rustling in the orchard, and through the cherry-trees Jinny Jones herself came running, her finger on her lips.

'Hush, Tom Tiddler!' she called softly. When she got close to the gate she pressed her face against it, and said, 'Oh, Tom, is it really you?'

'Yes, it is,' said Tom. 'Let me in!'

'I can't,' said Jinny Jones. 'Gogmagog keeps the key on a chain round his neck. He is asleep just now, but he wakes at the least touch. While he sleeps we have to strip one of the cherry-trees ready for his next meal. Oh, Tom! He has eaten up nearly all the cherries in the garden, and when he has eaten the cherries he is going to eat *us*! Luckily he likes cherries even better than little girls. Oh, Tom, whatever are we going to do?'

'Before the cherries are done,' said Tom, 'I'll find a way in, and kill him.'

'You can't,' said Jinny Jones. 'Nobody can.' And then she told Tom this story.

When Gogmagog was a baby, just like any other baby, his Mother woke up one Monday morning in the thick of a London fog; and she had no milk to put in his bottle, because the milk-boy had missed his way. So carrying her baby in a shawl over her back, she set out to the West, hoping to meet with a cow. But if she met one, the fog was too heavy for her to see it, and by evening she was tired out, and her baby was still hungry. Presently through the fog she saw a gleam of light, which came from a pool of golden water, as bright as the sun itself. Standing round the pool were six Bay Mares, with coats and manes of gold. They were ten times as big as any horse she had ever seen before. She was afraid to go near the giant Mares, and hid herself and her baby under a bush near by.

Before long there came a clatter of hoofs through the fog, and a seventh great Bay Mare ran panting to the pool; but the coat of this one was dingy and stained, and its shining mane was tangled.

She lay down by the water and said, 'Oh, sisters, what a day I've had! From morning till night I have dragged the Chariot of the Sun through the fog, choking every inch of the way, and see now what a state I'm in! What wouldn't I give to have my coat and mane combed sleek and smooth again!'

At this Gogmagog's Mother took her courage in her hands and stepped out from the bush, saying, 'I will wash your coat with my own hands, and sleek your mane with my own comb, if you will give me drink for my baby.'

'Do so!' said the Mare.

Gogmagog's Mother took the kerchief from her neck, dipped it in the water, and washed all the grime from the Mare's golden coat. Then she took the comb from her hair, and combed the tangles out of the Mare's golden mane. The Mare thanked her, and said, 'Now milk me until the bottle is full. When your child has drunk of my milk, he will never be able to die on a Monday, for I myself have drunk of the water of the Sun, and it is I who every Monday draw the Sun's Chariot from East to West.'

Gogmagog's Mother did as she was told. No sooner had the baby taken its bottle of mare's milk than it grew to twice its former size. On Tuesday the fog was as heavy as ever, and Tuesday's Mare returned at the day's end as bedraggled as Monday's. She too offered the Mother her milk in return for a combing. The Mother washed and combed her till she glittered like gold, and then gave her baby its Tuesday bottle; after which the baby became twice as big as before.

Now the fog lasted for a whole week, so by Sunday night Gogmagog had drunk the milk of the seven golden Bays that draw the Sun, and had become a giant. In consequence of all this, there was no day of the week on which he could be killed.

'So when people talk of killing him,' said Jinny Jones, 'Gogmagog only laughs and says, "Let them try." Oh, Tom!' cried she, 'what *can* be done to him?'

'Nothing,' said Jerry, 'nothing at all. Let's go and have breakfast.'

'*Can't* anything be done to Gogmagog, Simon?' asked Tom.

'Gogmagog can neither be killed nor hurt,' said Simon, 'but he can be imprisoned. And the only prison that is strong enough to hold him is the Leaden Hall in the heart of London. If once you can get him inside it and lock the door, he will never be able to get out again. Unfortunately the key of the door is lost, and nobody can make another but the Smith who lives in a field.'

'Come along, Simon! Come along, Jerry!' cried

Tom. 'We must go at once and find the Smith in the Field. Good-bye, Jinny Jones!'

'Good-bye, Tom Tiddler,' said Jinny Jones. 'Be sure you come back before Gogmagog has eaten all the cherries.'

8

THE SMITH'S FIELD

LONG BEFORE TOM reached the Field he heard the Smith at work, for the clank of his anvil was as loud as the bells of St. Paul's, and rang out for miles around. In between the clanks came the sound of mighty groans, as though somebody's heart was bursting with sorrow. Led by these noises, Tom soon found the Field. It had a deep ditch all round it, and outside the ditch prowled several figures in black masks and cloaks. It was plain to see they were Villains. In the middle of the Field stood the forge; and by the light of the red fire within, Tom saw the Smith himself. He was a tall strong man, with great muscles on his arms that were bared to the shoulder. When he struck the red-hot iron, he swung his hammer as though he could crack the anvil in two. Every now and then between the blows he stepped outside, shook his fist at the Villains, looked into the Ditch, groaned aloud, and returned to his work.

On seeing Tom approach, he paused with his hammer in the air, and called, 'Hi, youngster! Do you happen to have seen a Hound anywhere about?'

'No,' said Tom. 'Have you lost one?'

'I have,' said the Smith. 'He lived in that Ditch, and I've had him from a pup, ever since I first became Smith to King Lud of London, and began to forge his Gates. For Gates is a craze with King Lud, there's no end to the Gates he wants made. Palace Gates and Prison Gates, Park Gates and Garden Gates, a Gate for his Bishops, a Gate for his Aldermen, a New Gate, an Old Gate, a High Gate, and all! And it's only me can make them to suit him. Whenever a Gate's done I carry it on my back to King Lud, and he tells me where to set it up. While I'm away, my hound watches the forge, and keeps off the Villains, who come round to steal my iron. But a week ago he heard a bleating of sheep passing by, and there was no keeping him. Out of the Ditch he jumped, and I haven't seen him since.'

'Have you looked for him?' asked Tom.

'How can I?' said the Smith. 'So sure as I leave my Forge the Villains will steal my iron. Here's this Gate, now, which King Lud has just ordered me to make for Mr. Billing, the Royal Fishmonger. It's not done yet, and when it is done how I shall get it to the Palace beats *me*, without my Hound to leave on guard. You're sure you haven't seen my Hound, youngster?'

'Sure,' said Tom.

'A black Hound,' said the Smith.

'No,' said Tom.

'With red eyes,' persisted the Smith.

'No,' said Tom.

'And a stumpy tail,' urged the Smith.

'No,' said Tom.

'Then what have *you* come for?' asked the Smith.

'To get a new key to open the Leaden Hall,' said Tom; and told him all the story of Gogmagog and Jinny Jones.

The Smith listened attentively, leaning on his hammer. When Tom had done, he said,

'Fair's fair, youngster. I'll make you a key if you'll find me my Hound, and I can't say fairer than that.'

'But I'm in a hurry,' said Tom.

'And so am I,' said the Smith.

'Look here,' said Tom, 'make me the key now, and I'll give you Jerry for a watch-dog . . . I mean a watch-goat.'

'Is he clever and faithful?' asked the Smith.

'We-ell,' said Tom, who was a truthful boy. He looked round for Jerry, and saw him standing by the Ditch, eating grass from the hand of one of the Villains on the other side. So Tom said, 'Have Simon, then. He's a splendid Watch-Owl, and catches mice by the dozen.'

'Have you ever seen him catch a man?' asked the Smith.

'We-ell,' said Tom again.

'No,' said the Smith, 'it must be as I say. Bring me my Hound, and I'll make you your key. And good-day to you.'

Tom turned away sorrowfully, wondering where to seek first for the Smith's Hound. He looked at Simon, sitting on his shoulder, but Simon seemed to be asleep.

'Simon!' said Tom.

But Simon didn't budge.

'Wake up, lazy!' cried Tom, and pulled at his feathers.

Then Simon opened one eye and said, 'Am I never going to get my nap in peace? Don't you know I need my sleep by day as much as you need your sleep by night?'

'Oh, but, Simon,' said Tom, 'you do know everything, don't you?'

'I know one thing,' said Simon, 'I want my nap.'

'You shall have your nap,' said Tom, 'if you'll tell me where the Smith's Hound is. But if you're going to be a cross old Owl and say nothing, I'll pull your tail every time you shut your eyes.'

'A lot of good *you* are, aren't you?' muttered Simon. 'What would you do without me, pray? And yet you were going to give me away to that big brown Smith for a Watch-Owl. A Watch-Owl! Me!'

'Oh, *that's* what's ruffled you, is it?' said Tom. 'You might remember it was all for Jinny Jones.'

'Well, well,' said Simon, 'I shall have to help you once more, I see. The Smith's Hound has followed the Shepherd who lives under a Bush; and now pray don't disturb me any more.'

He shut his eyes and sank his head in his feathers as though he meant business; while Tom, full of glee again, shouted to Jerry to come after him, and went off at the top of his speed to find the Shepherd's Bush.

9

THE SHEPHERD'S BUSH

IT WAS A lovely day, and London was full of green leaves and sunshine. As he ran, Tom heard the notes of a pipe and the bleating of lambs mingling with the light and the dancing leaves of London. Following these sounds he soon came to a Bush as big as a bower, covered with pink blossoms. Under it sat the Shepherd, piping his tune, and at his feet lay a big black Hound with red eyes and a stumpy tail, which he wagged in time to the music. All around were the sheep, leaping and dancing. Everything seemed happy except the Shepherd, whose blue eyes were full of tears, which flowed quietly down his cheeks as he piped his tune.

'Dear me!' cried Tom Tiddler, 'whatever is amiss with you this beautiful day?'

The Shepherd did not answer until he came to the end of his tune; then he laid down his pipe and said, 'I have lost my Lass. The dullest day is beautiful when you have your Lass, and the fairest day is dull when she is lost.'

As he spoke the Shepherd looked so sorrowful that Tom quite forgot he had come to chide him for stealing the Smith's Hound, and said, 'Tell me your story.'

'I was born in London Fields,' said the Shepherd, 'and while I was still young was made prentice to the Shepherd who lived here before me. Now there are few spots in London lonelier than this; for miles around there is nothing but meadows and copses, and this Bush in their midst. And for company there are the sheep and their lambs. The Old Shepherd had no dog, and I served him in that way as well as in others. He was a silent man, who never spoke at all. He would point with his finger if he meant me to go, and beckon with it if he meant me to come. He nodded his head for Yes, and shook it for No. He frowned when he was angry, and smiled when he was pleased. By these means we came to understand each other very well. One morning I found him lying under the Bush, with one eye open and one eye shut. As soon as I came to his side he handed me his crook, closed his other eye, and opened it and its fellow no more. In this way I became the Shepherd of the Bush, and by the death of the Old One had even less company than before. I knew I needed a boy as he had done, but did not know where to find one. To help me bear the extra loneliness I made this pipe, and taught myself to play a tune on it. It gave pleasure to the sheep and lambs as well as to myself, and when I piped they danced. One day as I was piping I saw something dancing in that copse yonder, and ran to look, for it appeared to be taller than any sheep I had ever seen. What was my surprise to see a boy, all dressed in brown rags, with a bunch of lavender in his hat which he held on with both hands.

'Shepherd,' said he, 'you pipe the sweetest tune in all the streets of London.'

'Boy,' said I, 'will you stay with me and watch my sheep?'

'Yes, for a penny a day,' said he, 'and a tune when I come and another when I go.' And so it was arranged. Each morning he came and danced before the Bush; each day he watched my sheep and earned his penny; and each evening danced before the Bush, and went. Where he came from and where he went to I never knew. Nor why, when he danced, he always held his hat on with both hands. What this meant for me in the way of company you may guess; I had never even talked with any one before, and this was a sweet lad besides.

'Now two weeks ago as I was playing in the evening, and he and the lambs were dancing, it rained and shone together, and a rainbow appeared. At sight of it the lambs leaped twice as high for joy, and so did my

Boy, at the same time throwing his hands out as though to catch it. With this motion his hat fell off, and over his shoulders rolled a wealth of golden hair. I cried out with astonishment, and the boy turned as red as a rose. He cast me one glance and fled through the trees. From that hour to this I have not seen him – or rather, her, for it was now plain to me that this was not only a lass, but the only Lass for me. I have wandered all round London playing my pipe in the hope of drawing her to me, but in vain. A week ago, however, this Hound ran after me and for love of my music attached itself to me; and very glad I am of its help and company. But it cannot take the place of my Lass, who is gone for ever.' And the Shepherd wiped his tears, which were beginning to flow again.

'I am sorry for you,' said Tom, 'but that Hound belongs to the Smith in the Field, and I have come to fetch him home.'

'I will never let him go,' said the Shepherd, 'until I have my Lass again. Find her for me, and you are welcome to the Hound. And please call off your goat, who is annoying my sheep.'

'Jerry, come here!' cried Tom, 'and advise me what to do.'

'Do?' said Jerry. 'Why do anything? It is very pleasant here, and the grass is plentiful.'

'Simon,' begged Tom, 'what shall I do to find the Shepherd's Lass?'

'The Lass lives on Lavender Hill,' said Simon 'and there you must go to find her.'

So off went Tom like the wind to Lavender Hill.

10

THE LASS OF
LAVENDER HILL

AS HE RAN with Simon on his shoulder and Jerry at
his heels, Tom's nose was assailed by the sweetest of
perfumes, and following the scent he soon came in sight
of a hill. And a pretty sight it was; from top to bottom it
was covered with lavender bushes in full bloom, and all
round the hill went pretty girls, kneeling and stooping,
and gathering the stalks. When their baskets were full
they took them up the hill and emptied their loads at
the feet of a handsome young fellow who sat on the top,
tying them in bunches of sixteen blue branches to the
bunch.

'Deary me!' said Tom. 'How amongst so many lasses
shall I ever find the Shepherd's Lass?'

'It can't be done,' said Jerry, 'so why bother to try?'
And he began to munch the lavender, well content.

'You had better ask the boy on the hilltop,' said
Simon, closing one eye. Up the hill Tom trudged,
passing many pretty girls dressed in lavender linen; but
as he drew near the top he saw that the boy sitting there

was dressed in brown rags, and had golden curls flowing over his shoulders.

'Good-day,' said Tom. 'Are you not the Lass who helped the Shepherd under the Bush?'

'I am,' she confessed. 'What of him?'

'I have come to tell you,' said Tom, 'that he is very unhappy, and will not be otherwise until you go back to him.'

'Lack-a-daisy!' cried the Lass, 'How can I go back to him dressed like this? As long as he took me for a boy it did not matter; but now that he has found me out, I cannot go back to him without my petticoat.'

'Then why don't you put on your petticoat?' asked Tom.

'La!' said she, tossing her golden curls, 'that's easier said than done. Three weeks ago I sent it to the wash, with my best bodice and cap; and all that came back was this suit of rags. When I send word to the Laundress by one of my friends, all she answers is that the petticoat is mislaid, but she will send it next week. Now see what a plight I am in! For you must know that this is the Lavender Hill of King Lud, and we are his Lavender Girls. It is our duty each week to take him the lavender we have gathered to put among his linen, and for this he pays us a penny a day, and a currant bun to eat on Sunday. But since I have only these old rags to wear, I am ashamed to show myself at the Palace. I could report the Laundress to the King, of course, but that would get her into trouble; and dear knows there's trouble enough in the world already without making more. So for three weeks I have had to miss my wages and my currant bun, and for want of a job I took service with the Shepherd. Now, alack! I've lost that job too, and all through dancing my hair down. No, I will never go back to him without my petticoat!'

'Where does the Laundress live?' asked Tom.

'In Petticoat Lane, to be sure!' said the Lass.

'What was your Petticoat like?' asked Tom.

'It was sprigged with lavender from top to hem,' said the Lass.

'If I fetch you your petticoat,' said Tom, 'will you promise to go back to the Shepherd?'

'If you fetch my petticoat,' said the Lass, 'I will run to him as fast as my heels can fly.'

'That's a bargain!' said Tom. And dragging Jerry off the lavender bushes, he set out without more ado for Petticoat Lane.

11

PETTICOAT LANE

PRESENTLY AS TOM ran the air became thick with steam, mixed with a strong smell of soapsuds. Led by these signs, Tom soon reached a big square yard, with lanes running out of it on all sides. Down the lanes he could see endless rows of washing-lines and clothes-pegs, with garments of all sorts fluttering from them. In the middle of the yard was an open shed, consisting of an immense red roof held up by four stout posts. Round the four sides of the shed ran a wooden bench on which stood a hundred green washtubs, with a hundred sturdy washerwomen at work. The steam rose in clouds from the tubs as the women scrubbed and rubbed and wrung the linen, which they afterwards rinsed in a fountain in the middle of the shed. Tom saw that each of the hundred washtubs held something different: in one were the sheets, in another the towels, in a third the table-cloths, and in a fourth the pocket-handkerchiefs. One woman had all the shirts, and her neighbour all the collars. And all the while the big plump women washed, a little bony woman ran round and round the benches, poking her sharp nose into every tub, chattering, scolding, and saying a dozen things at once.

'Bustle, girls, bustle! Don't stop to talk! Betsy, Betsy! don't scrub the King's sheets so hard! you'll scrub holes in 'em. Now Doll, be careful do with the Earl's lace ruffles – if you should tear 'em he'll clap you in prison! Priscilla, where's the Beefeater's best handkerchief, the one with the bull's head worked in the corner? Have you lost it? If you have, he'll eat you instead of a Sirloin for his Sunday dinner! Grizzle! how many aprons came to the Wash this week? What! only nine thousand three hundred and two? You had better count 'em again to be sure. Now bustle, bustle, bustle, or we'll never get done by tea-time! Well, little boy, what do *you* want?'

'If you please,' said Tom, 'I've come for the sprigged petticoat of the Lass of Lavender Hill, which was lost in the Wash three weeks ago.'

'Drat the Lass!' snapped the little bony woman. 'Will she never stop bothering me?' Then she cried out, 'Barbara! has that sprigged petticoat turned up this week?'

'No, Missus,' said Barbara from her washtub full of petticoats. 'There's quilted petticoats, and flounced petticoats, and frilled petticoats, and striped petticoats, but never a sprigged one in all the tub. Maybe it's on the drying-line in Petticoat Lane.'

'Come along o' me and look for yourself,' said the Missus, and she led Tom down one of the lanes where thousands of petticoats were hanging out to dry. Up and down ran Tom, amongst the white lace petticoats, the green silk petticoats and those of calico, lawn, and dimity – but not a sign of a lavender-sprigged petticoat could he see.

'I can't find it,' said Tom.

'Then you must go back without it,' said the Missus, 'and tell her it's mislaid but is sure to turn up.'

'I can't do that either,' said Tom.

'Why not?' snapped the Missus.

'Because if I do,' said Tom, 'Gogmagog the Giant will eat up all the little girls in London.'

'Lackadaisydiddle!' cried the Missus, throwing up her skinny hands. 'And all for want of a lavender petticoat! If I'd ha' known it was as bad as that, I'd ha' told the truth three weeks ago.'

'Never mind,' said Tom hopefully, 'tell it now.'

'Ah, it's all very well to talk cheerful,' said the Missus, 'but it won't help you much. Now it was like this. Four weeks ago one of my women started sneezing, and I sent her home to bed; so come Saturday, when we do the sorting, there was I short-handed. Just then I saw a sort of a creature hanging about the Yard, dressed in brown sacking all in rags—'

'What sort of a sort of a creature?' asked Tom.

'Well,' said the Missus, ''twas about fifteen years old, I should fancy, but whether 'twas girl or boy I couldn't say. However, it had a pair of useful hands, so I called out – D'ye want a job? And it called back, Yus!'

'Yes?' said Tom.

'No, Yus I said, for Yus *it* said. It was a poor sort of creature. However, I gave it a penny and pushed over the basket of petticoats and told it to sort 'em out in separate piles – those for King Lud's Court, those for the Lavender Girls, those for the Market-Women, and so forth. Then I went off to see to other matters, and when I came back I found all the petticoats in their proper heaps, and the creature gone. I thought no more about it, but delivered the petticoats where they belonged; and the next thing I heard was that the Lavender Lass had got a suit of brown rags in place of what she'd sent. So I suppose the creature took it. But where to look for it *I* don't know, I'm sure. I can only say this much, that if you recover the petticoat and bring it back, I'll wash it and starch it and iron it with my own hands, and send it straight to the Lass, though it be on a Wednesday or Thursday!'

As the Missus finished her tale, there came a great

clatter and shrieking from the yard, and running back they saw Jerry dancing round the benches, butting over the tubs one by one, and enjoying himself hugely, while the soapsuds ran all over the place, and the clothes fell into the gutters, and the Washerwomen screamed.

'Shoo!' cried the Missus, flapping her apron at Jerry. 'Shoo! get down, you great nasty beast! Drat your goat, and drat *you*!' she snapped at Tom. 'There's all the day's work to be done over again!'

Still flapping her apron, she shooed Tom and Jerry and Simon out of the yard.

'Whatever made you behave like that?' demanded Tom, when they were at a safe distance.

'He, he, he! the buckets tipped over so nicely,' chuckled Jerry. 'Who could help it? And then the women screamed and jumped about. He, he, he! where's your sense of humour?'

'*Your* sense of humour will be the end of us, one of these days,' said Simon.

'And however am I to find the creature now?' said Tom. 'The Missus is so cross, it's no use asking *her*.'

'Then ask somebody else,' said Simon.

'Dear Simon, do tell me! What's the creature's name?'

'Wormwood.'
'And where does it live?'
'In the Royal Slums.'
So off went Tom on his search anew.

12

WORMWOOD

NOW AS TOM ran, his ears began to be troubled with a mixture of sounds, such as a scrapey scraping sound, and a sloppy slopping sound, and a clattery clattering sound, but most troublesome of all was a muttery muttering sound that sounded very unhappy indeed. As he drew nearer he could hear the words in the mutter, and they went something like this:

'Oh-dear-oh-dear! I shall never git it clean! Oh-dear-oh-dear! wot a big place London is to be sure, and wot a lot of dirt there is in it! It's more than one creature's job to scrub it all, I do say. There goes another scrubbing-brush! Oh-dear-oh-dear, that ever I was born! I shall never-never-*never* git it clean!'

Turning a corner, Tom came out of the broad street into a narrow alley. He had to pass under an archway to enter it, and over the archway hung a sign with a crown on it, but the gilt of the crown was tarnished and chipped, and in a very sorry state. The alley was as dark as it was narrow, and was paved with big uneven cobbles. Half-way down it Tom saw a little figure on its hands and knees, with a big pail of water by its side, and in the pail a long-handled mop. Piled up on one side was a heap of new scrubbing-brushes with only the backs left. The bristles had all been worn off with scrubbing. The little figure, which was clothed only in an old brown sack, was staring dismally at the back of a scrubbing-brush which it had just worn out. Its face was so dirty, and so hung about with matted hair, that Tom could hardly see what its features were like; he could only see its two big eyes staring through the tangled locks.

As he approached, the figure held up the brush and said, 'See that now! That's the eleventh I've worn out this morning, and the place is no cleaner than it was when I began. Oh-dear-oh-dear, that ever I was born!'

'What a horrid place this is,' said Tom. 'Why do you stop in it?'

'I dunno,' said the little figure. 'It's where I was put.'

'Is your name Wormwood?'

'That's me, and this is the Royal Slums, where all the dirt is shoved. It's my job to scrub it out, but day in day out, scrub as I will, I can't get it clean, though I wear my fingers down to the bone and the bristles down to the roots. I'm King Lud's scullion and odd-jobber, you see, and when I'm not scrubbing his stones,

I'm scrubbing his sinks and pots, oh–dear–oh–dear!'

'How awful,' said Tom. 'Are you a girl or a boy?'

'Never thought about it,' said Wormwood, throwing away the old scrubbing–brush, and taking a new one from the heap by the wall. 'Wall, I must git on with it – no time to rest.'

'Don't you *ever* have a rest?' asked Tom.

'Two hours on Saturday, and four times a year on Bank Holidays.'

'And what do you do then?'

'I mostly sleeps,' said Wormwood. 'But *larst* Bank Holiday I had a Beano. It was like this. There's a chap I know called Arry who brings the King's cabbages once a week, and spares me an old sack now and again to dress myself in. Well, a month ago he sez to me, Next Monday's Bank Holiday, he sez; you put on your best togs, and I'll drive you in me donkey–cart to Ampstead, and we'll have a Beano. Then he goes away, and I didn't know what to do, for I hadn't any best togs to put on, and I couldn't disgrace Arry by going to Ampstead in one of his own cabbage–sacks. But oh, I did so want a Beano! So on Saturday afternoon I went to the Laundry where all the clothes are washed, and the Missus give me a penny to help sort 'em, and while I was sorting 'em I saw the prettiest petticoat you can think of, and a bodice and cap to go with it. So when nobody was looking I slipped round the corner and put them on, and then I crept back quick and shoved my old brown rags into the middle of the bundle of petticoats, and ran off as fast as I could. And on Bank Holiday,' said Wormwood, with sparkling eyes, 'on Bank Holiday, instead of scrubbing London I scrubbed meself, and put on the petticoat, and had a Beano with Arry.'

'Hurrah!' cried Tom. 'That's the very petticoat I've come for, and if you'll give it back to me I promise you no one will scold you, and as soon as I can I'll bring you a new petticoat of your very own!'

But Wormwood's big eyes filled with tears, and Wormwood's mouth turned down and down till it could turn no farther.

'Oh-dear-oh-dear!' said Wormwood. 'I'll give you the petticoat, but I don't know whatever you'll say when you see it.'

Wormwood scuttled down the alley, felt behind a stack of old scrubbing-brushes, and came back with what had once been a pretty petticoat of fine lawn sprigged with lavender. But now it was torn to ribbons so that they hardly hung together.

'However did that happen?' cried Tom in dismay.

'It was such a Beano, you see,' explained Wormwood. 'And what with the merry-go-rounds and the sliding mats, and Arry and the crowd, and the hawthorns catching at you, and the Bull in the Bush ripping up everything in sight, by the time I got back this was all that was left. It *was* a Beano!'

'I should have liked to be there,' observed Jerry, licking his lips, 'and help to rip things up. How did the Bull do it – like this?'

And before Tom could stop him he had put down his head, caught the petticoat on his horns, and tossed and tousled it till it fell in shreds at his feet. Then Tom fell on *him* and beat him angrily with his fists.

'You *wicked* goat!' he cried. 'However can I take them back to the Lavender Lass now? They were bad enough before, but now they are quite past mending.'

'Yes,' said Simon, cocking his head on one side, 'they're as near past mending as they can be. In fact, I know only one sempstress clever enough to make them as good as new again.'

'Oh, who?' cried Tom.

'The Old Lady of Threadneedle Street, of course.'

'Where's Threadneedle Street?'

'By the bank where the new mint grows.'

'Good-bye, Wormwood!' cried Tom. 'Let me take these torn things away, and when they are mended and Jinny Jones is saved, you shall have a whole dress of your own, of any colour you like!'

And off he ran again, full of new hope, while Wormwood went back to the slopping of water, the clattering of pails, and the scrubbing of the London stones.

13

THE OLD LADY OF THREADNEEDLE STREET

AS SOON AS he stepped outside the archway, Tom drew a deep breath of fresh air to get rid of the fusty musty smell of the dirt in the Royal Slums. He thought he had never smelled air so sweet before; and somewhere far away at the back of his deep breath he got a refreshing whiff of mint, mingled with the scent of gardens. This was good enough for Tom; so taking one deep breath after another, he went in the direction of the scent, and as he went each breath became still fuller of the fragrance of herbs and flowers. In due course he reached the bank where the Old Lady sat plying her needle. It was a beautiful deep green bank, and bloomed with mint all the way up. At the bottom the mint was of copper-colour, half-way up its leaves were silver, but the mint at the top had leaves of the purest gold. People of all sorts wandered about the bank, gathering the mint; some in poor clothes contented themselves with stooping for the copper mint at the foot of the bank; midway were gentlefolk in good garments, picking the silver; and on the top of the bank walked noblemen in rich array, gathering up the gold.

Opposite the bank lay a great garden in which grew nothing but stocks of many colours, white, rose, and purple. Some were flourishing, and others were not doing so well. Among the richest borders wandered a gardener, who, to Tom's surprise, was not a man, but a handsome Bull. He carried a watering-can and a pair of garden-scissors; he seemed to know just the right moment to cut the flowers to the best advantage, and very often those he watered doubled in size the moment after. But behind him ambled a shaggy old Bear, whose object it seemed to be to destroy the stocks, and it was where he trampled the borders that the flowers were poorest.

At the foot of the bank, facing the Stock-garden, sat the Old Lady herself. She was so ample that her skirts spread all around the stool she sat on, and Tom could not see what sort of a seat supported her at all; but it was evidently a very firm one. At her feet was her cushion, stuck with thousands of needles like a porcupine, on her right hand was a gigantic spool of thread, and on her left hand a vast basket stuffed with a mountain of needlework, which she was stitching and patching. The clothes she made and mended were of all sorts, here a

French glove, and there a Dutch bonnet, now a Spanish shawl, and then an Italian cloak; German aprons, Japanese sashes, Indian scarves, and English smocks and socks and caps and gowns – the Old Lady had her needle in them all. Her fingers flew faster than the eye could follow, you never saw such work as she put into the things – she could mend the raggedest tear so that it was as good as new, and while she kept one eye on the work in hand, the other seemed to glance all round her head for the new work coming in. For from all sides people came running to her with jobs to be done, or with needles they wanted her to thread from her spool so that they could do their jobs for themselves. She satisfied them all, as soon as they had paid their fee. Tom had to wait his turn, but it came at last, and he found himself standing before her with his shreds of lavender lawn in his hands.

'Well, well, well,' said the Old Lady, 'and what have you there, little boy?' But before he could answer she had taken the bits from his hand and held them up to the light, saying, 'I see, I see, I see. Yes, that's a job to be sure, and no mistake.'

'Can you mend them, ma'am?' asked Tom.

'Mend them? yes!' said the Old Lady. 'I can mend anything except torn hearts. My needle's no good for that sort of a tear. But come now, where's your Saturday Penny?'

gates. The Bull now pushed Jerry before him, locked the gates, and rolling his red eyes at Tom roared, 'Jump up!'

'On your back?' asked Tom.

'Just so,' said the Bull, 'and make your goat do likewise.'

'But where are you taking us?' asked Tom.

'Where you'll do me and my stocks no more mischief,' bellowed the Bull. 'Jump up!'

Tom still hung back, but Simon whispered in his ear, 'You can't do better. He'll take you just where you'll find what you want.'

Without more ado Tom jumped on to the Bull's back, Jerry clambered after, and off they went like the wind.

14

THE SPANIARD'S SWORD

GALLOP-A-GALLOP WENT the Bull through the streets of London Town, and bumpity-bump went Tom and Jerry on his back. Tom, who was in front, clutched the Bull's two horns, and held on like a brave lad, though now and then when the bone in the Bull's back came up a little too suddenly he couldn't help saying, 'Ow!' But Jerry, who sat behind with his two forelegs locked round Tom's waist, and his beard waving over Tom's right shoulder, kept up one long bleat of talk that never stopped.

'Oh mee-h! Oh mee-h! was ever a goat so shaken up before? Stop, Bull, stop, or you'll rattle my two horns out of their sockets! What has a nice quiet goat like me done to deserve it? Just munched a flower or so, where they wouldn't be missed. Stop swishing your tail, Bull, you're tickling my mid-rib! Did ever a nice quiet peaceable goat suffer the like? And what are flowers *for*, pray, if not to be munched? Would you have me munch sticks and stones? Oh me-h mee-h meee-h! what a bump!'

'Hold your tongue, Jerry!' gasped Tom, 'and don't wiggle your chin on my collar-bone. It hurts.'

'That's right!' mumbled Jerry. 'Blame me! Blame me for all. Was it me stole Jinny Jones away? Was it me would have chained you up with a golden chain? Was it me would have Bugsbied you? Was it me asked you to take a ride on a mad bull's back, that makes your insides feel like a sack of potatoes swinging on a roundabout? Was it me, eh, was it me-eeh?'

'Oh, do keep quiet,' begged Tom. 'Simon's not making a fuss.'

'Simon's got wings, and can go as he pleases,' said Jerry. 'If I'd got what Simon's got, I wouldn't be where I am.'

'If you'd got my wits instead of your dunderhead,' said Simon, 'you wouldn't need wings.'

'Oh, me-eh! Oh, mee-h!' bleated Jerry. 'Was ever a nice quiet peaceable lamb of a goat so spoken to before?'

'Look out!' warned Simon. For the Bull at last had stopped with a jerk that shot both Tom and Jerry over his head into the middle of a leafy bush. Jerry immediately opened his mouth and began to nibble the leaves, while Tom picked himself up, rubbed his elbows, and looked about him.

The Bush was very big and very round, and covered

with Seville oranges; it stood in the middle of a beautiful wild Heath, all ups and downs and hillocks and dingles, with glades of silver birch, and groves of pink crab-apple-trees, and reedy ponds and sandy creeks – a fine spot for games and hiding-places, Tom thought. As he gazed, he saw a flutter of red through the branches of the Bush, and running down one of the hillocks came the figure of a man, in a velvet coat and breeches glittering with gold embroidery. On his arm was a great red mantle that streamed in the wind. As soon as he saw the Bull he gave a shout, and ran at him with the mantle. The Bull put down his head and made a rush for the red cloth. But before he could rip it up, the man stepped aside, darted round the Bush, and then stopped to tease the Bull again with his fluttering cloak. Round and round the Bush they sported till both were tired. The man then folded his cloak, threw his arm over the Bull's neck, and moved off with him through the tree in as friendly a fashion as though he had been a horse or a dog.

'Who is he, and what was he doing?' asked Tom of Simon.

'He was having a game with the Bull,' said Simon, 'because he's a Spaniard.'

'A Spaniard!' shouted Tom gleefully. 'Come along, Jerry! I must catch him at once.'

Jerry gulped down an orange, and mumbled, 'Why

are you always so fond of saying Come-along? Stop-where-you-are suits *me*.'

But Tom was too eager to ask the Spaniard for his sword to listen. He ran out of the Bush in the direction in which the Spaniard and the Bull had vanished through the trees. They were no longer in sight. Soon, however, he heard the sound of music, and through the trees he saw another man approaching; he had a swarthy skin, gay clothes, a feather in his hat, and rings in his ears, and as he walked he twanged a guitar and hummed a tune. Seeing Tom he stopped, and said, 'Good-day, child.'

'Good-day, sir,' said Tom. 'Have you seen a Spaniard go by?'

The singer smiled, and his white teeth gleamed like pearls in his dark face. '*You* shall see a Spaniard go by,' said he, 'when I go by.'

'What,' cried Tom, 'are you a Spaniard too?'

'I am, child.'

'But, sir, you have no sword.'

'I had one once, when I left Spain,' said the Singer, 'but I changed it later for this guitar. The Old Lady offered it me for my steel, which she wanted for needles, and music is better than fighting, so I agreed.'

Tom's face fell. 'Then you're no good to me,' he said, 'for I must have a Spanish sword as soon as I can, or Gogmagog will eat up Jinny Jones. Where can I find the other Spaniard with the red cloak?'

'He is usually where the Bull is, and the Bull is where the Bush is,' said the Singer.

'He isn't there now,' said Tom.

'No matter,' said the Singer, 'for even if he were, he has no sword. He gave it up some time ago to the Old Lady, in exchange for the red cloak with which he sports with the Bull; for he loves sport even better than he loves fighting.'

'Then what am I to do for a Spanish sword?' said Tom in dismay.

The Singer strummed a chord and said, 'There is still a little hope, though I fear not much. You must know that there are three of us Spaniards dwelling on this Heath, which was given us by King Lud in exchange for the person of a tall and dangerous Moor who would have attempted his life. This Moor had conquered Spain, and wishing to conquer London next had sailed hither bringing with him me and my two brothers as his servants. We all felt shame to serve the conquering Moor, for we were of noble family, but my Eldest Brother felt it most of all. He it is to whom I will now take you, for he still possesses his sword, which is the very apple of his eye. He prefers it to both music and sport, and for what he will part with it I cannot think. However, we shall see.'

The Singer led the way across the Heath to the Spaniard's dwelling, a square white house with balconies hung with vines, and a courtyard with a fountain in the middle. Beside the fountain sat a tall proud man in black armour, inlaid with gold and silver. Across his knees lay his naked sword, of the finest blue steel. When he saw the Singer approaching with Tom, he lifted his haughty eyelids and said, 'Well, brother, is this boy the Earl's messenger, come at last?'

'No, brother,' said the Singer, 'this boy is his own messenger. He comes to make you a request.'

'Speak, boy!' commanded the Proud Spaniard.

Tom went straight up to him, laid his hand on his knee, and looking at him earnestly said, 'Sir, it's like this. The Old Lady wants a Spanish sword to make needles with.'

'Let her want!' cried the Spaniard, the blood rising in his swarthy cheek. 'The sword of an Hidalgo of Arragon is not steel for needles! Go, boy, before I thread your body with it! Ha!'

But Tom stood his ground and said again, 'Well, sir, it's like this. Until she has your sword she won't mend the petticoat, and the Lass won't go back to the Shepherd, and the Smith won't get his dog again, and there'll be no key to the Leaden Hall, and so Gogmagog the Giant will eat up Jinny Jones, and I am very fond of

Jinny Jones, sir.' And Tom looked still more earnestly into the Proud Spaniard's eyes.

The angry colour faded from the Spaniard's cheek, and laying his hand on Tom's he said, 'Say no more. If you are fond of Jinny Jones, all things must be sacrificed to save her, even the sword of an Hidalgo of Arragon. For love is better than sport, or music, or even fighting. Therefore you shall have my sword as soon as my friend the Earl is married. For I am to be his Best Man on this great occasion, and how can I appear at the Earl's Court without my sword? No, even for Jinny Jones I could not endure that shame!'

'When will the Earl be married, sir?' asked Tom.

'I expect his messenger hourly. I have expected him hourly for the past month. And still he does not come.'

'Then it looks as though something's wrong,' said Tom thoughtfully.

'It does indeed,' said the Proud Spaniard.

'Then I'd better see the Earl about it at once,' said Tom.

'The sooner the better,' said the Proud Spaniard.

'Come along, Simon! Come along, Jerry!' said Tom.

'There you go again!' grumbled Jerry. And there they went.

15

THE BAKERS' STREET

'SIMON,' SAID TOM, 'how am I to know the Earl when I see him?'

'To begin with,' said Simon, 'he is a man.'

'So is the Smith,' said Tom.

'To go on with,' said Simon, 'he has two arms, two legs, two eyes, two ears, and only one nose.'

'So has the Proud Spaniard,' said Tom.

'And to end up with,' said Simon, 'he is in love with a lady.'

'So is the Shepherd,' said Tom. 'It seems to me that an Earl is very much like all other men I've ever seen.'

'I dare say he is,' said Simon; 'so you had better present yourself at his Court, and pick him out.'

'I will,' said Tom. 'Where is it?'

'I've answered quite enough questions for this time,' said Simon, 'and I'm going to sleep.' Which he did on the spot.

Tom scratched his head, and went on walking the way he was going, because it was as likely a way as any other. Presently, he became aware that instead of walking upon grass or gravel or stones, he was treading in a soft white dust that proved to be flour. The road was as thick with it as with snow in winter, and it made very pleasant walking indeed. As he went, kicking it up, and powdering himself from head to foot, he found that it grew deeper and deeper, until he reached a point where it was swept in great drifts against the sides of the houses. Inside the houses and indeed in the street itself, everybody was very busy. Men in white caps and aprons were bustling about, bringing out bundles of sacks, shovelling the flour into them, and piling them on carts which were driven off as fast as they were laden. A burly man with big arms was directing all the work.

'Careful, lads, careful!' he was saying. 'More flour there, John, and be quick about it. Ralph, load that next wagon with icing sugar, and don't stop to lick your fingers. George, count twenty thousand eggs into the lorry, and mind you don't crack a single shell. Bert, fill a thousand cans with cream, and mind you don't spill a single drop. Careful, now, but quick, for when this job's done there's the Earl's Wedding-Cake to bake.'

At these words Tom's heart gave a leap.

'Excuse me, sir,' he said politely, 'but is all this for the Earl's Wedding Breakfast?'

'Yes, my lad,' said the Head Baker, which is what the

burly man was. 'This morning I got orders to send to the Earl's Court, flour and eggs and almonds and cream and icing sugar in such quantities that it will take all the stores in the Baker's street to supply them. And I am to follow after with my twelve best Bakers to make the Wedding Cake. He must be going to invite all London to his wedding. But there, I've no time to gossip. George, have you got that twenty thousand eggs counted yet? Then now count me fifty thousand almonds, and look sharp about it – but careful, mind, careful!'

He turned away, and Tom saw that he would spare no more time for talk. So watching his opportunity, he hopped into a van that was being loaded with sugar, and stowed himself and Simon behind a bulging bag. Jerry jumped in beside him, and they were all so white with flour that Ralph never noticed them when he tumbled the next load of sugar-bags into the van. There they crouched till the van was full, and rumbled away towards the Earl's Court. Jerry soon ripped a hole in the nearest bag and licked up the sugar as it trickled out, and Tom himself wasn't above wetting his finger and dipping it into the stream of sweet stuff. Simon, who was superior to sugar, was either asleep or pretending to be.

16

THE EARL'S COURT

THE VAN RUMBLED on and on till Tom said, 'I do believe it is going on for ever.'

'Worse things could happen,' observed Jerry, who had emptied one sugar-bag, and was now ripping up another.

'If it doesn't stop soon, you'll be sick,' said Tom.

'It's worth it,' said Jerry.

However, before he had finished the second bag, the van pulled up, and people came to unload it. While the bags were being stacked beside the back door, Tom and Jerry crawled out and slipped round to the front of the building, which was a very grand place indeed, with white marble pillars leading into a great Court hung with silken cloths fringed with gold. The Earl's arms were embroidered on the cloths, and the Earl himself sat on a dais with a canopy over his head. He was a charming young man, in white satin clothes, trimmed with silver lace, and he had a rose stuck behind his ear.

In the Court was a stream of people who passed

before him in single file. The Earl's Steward announced the name of each comer; the Earl leaned forward eagerly, and asked a question; some reply was given; and at each reply the Earl sank back hopelessly in his seat, waved his hand in dismissal, and a newcomer took the place of the old. Tom fell in line with the rest, and saw this pantomime repeated many times. At last there were only two people in front of him; one had a golden postman's hat on his head, the other wore a silver tape-measure round his neck.

'The Postmaster-General from St. Martin-le-Grand!' announced the Steward, in a pompous voice; and the man in the gold hat bowed to the Earl.

'Ah, my dear Postmaster!' cried the Earl, leaning forward, 'what is *your* suggestion?'

'I suggest, my lord,' said the Postmaster-General, 'that you might stick it all over with white stamp-paper.'

The Earl sank back in his seat. 'It has been tried,' he sighed, 'and the rain always washes it off.' He waved his hand, and the Postmaster-General passed on.

'The Haberdasher-in-Chief from Haberdashers' Row,' announced the Steward. And up stepped the man with the silver tape-measure round his neck.

'Welcome, my dear Chief Haberdasher!' exclaimed the Earl, leaning forward again. 'And what is *your* bright idea?'

'My lord,' said the Haberdasher-in-Chief, 'it occurred to me that you might cover it entirely with white book-muslin at eleven-three the yard.'

But the Earl shook his head sadly. 'That too has been tried,' he said, 'and the wind always tears it to shreds.' And he sank back with a wave of his hand.

It was now Tom's turn.

'Name, please!' said the Steward.

'Tom Tiddler,' said Tom.

'Where from?' asked the Steward.

'Nowhere in particular,' said Tom.

So the Steward announced in his pompous tones:

'Tom Tiddler, from Nowhere in Particular!'

At the sight of Tom, Simon, and Jerry, plastered with sugar and flour, the Earl bounded up from his seat.

'Bless me, Tom Tiddler!' cried the Earl. 'How white you are! And what have you come to suggest?'

'If you please, my lord,' said Tom, 'I came to suggest that you should get married to-day.'

'A splendid suggestion!' said the Earl. 'Unfortunately, my lady is so particular that there's no pleasing her over a certain point she insists on.'

'What *is* the point?' asked Tom.

'Well, you must know that my Lady is the Lady of Limehouse, and though it is quite a little house, it is as white as lime can make it. She so loves its whiteness that she will only consent to be married in a chapel as white as her house. I know of an excellent chapel for the purpose, but unfortunately the London weather has soiled and stained it to such a degree that no one can remember if it ever was white to begin with, for it certainly isn't white now.'

'Then why not whiten it at once?' asked Tom.

'That's just it,' said the Earl. 'All the lime in London is in the possession of some one who will not part with it for love or money. I have tried to whiten the Chapel by every other means I can think of, and every day people flock to me with suggestions which all prove useless. But I must say, Tom Tiddler, that, always excepting my Lady's white house, I have never in my life seen anything quite so white as you are. How did you manage it?'

'Flour,' said Tom.

'And sugar,' said Jerry.

'Where are these things?' asked the Earl.

'In your own back-yard,' said Tom.

'Huzza!' cried the Earl. 'Why didn't I think of it before?' And he rushed to the back-yard followed by Tom. There they found the Head Baker and his twelve men, helping to unload the last of the wagons. The Head Baker took off his cap, saying,

'Good-day to your Lordship. This is the flour for the

pastry, and the eggs for the cakes, and the sugar and cream for the meringues. The almonds were sent on ahead, and the currants and spice are following on behind, with a hogshead of vanilla, a ton of candied rose-leaves, a ton of crystallised violets, and a ton of silver comfits. Now if you'll kindly show us the way to the kitchen, we'll make a start.'

'So you shall!' cried the Earl, 'but not in the kitchen. No, you must bring all these things along to the Chapel in which I am to be married, and make a start there.'

The Head Baker scratched his head. 'My lord,' he objected, 'we can't ice the cake in the Chapel.'

'You are not to ice the cake,' said the Earl, 'you are to ice the Chapel itself.'

'Very good, my lord,' said the Burly Baker. He gave directions to his men, the sugar, the cream and the flour, the eggs and the almonds, were packed up again on the vans, the carts, the wagons, the drays, and the lorries, and off they all went to the Chapel that had to be whitened.

sword; and behind the Earl, holding up the long white cloak he had donned, walked Tom as his Page of Honour. Simon still sat on his shoulder, but Jerry was nowhere to be seen, though Tom had called him over and over again.

'Well, we can't wait,' said Tom, 'we'll have to do without him, Simon.'

'Don't be too sure,' said Simon.

The two processions met at the Chapel door, and as the Lady and the Earl took hands, the sun came out.

'Happy is the bride,' said the Proud Spaniard, 'that the sun shines on!'

But even as he said it, the Bride burst into tears. For the cream began to run, the icing to melt, and the whipped eggs to turn brown. Moreover, all the children in the city were munching blanched almonds as fast as they could pick them out, and inside the Chapel all the London sparrows were pecking at the flour; while both inside and out gambolled Jerry, devouring flour and sugar, almonds, eggs and cream in great mouthfuls.

The Earl cried anxiously, 'Dry your tears, dear love! the White Friar is waiting to marry us.'

But the little lady stamped her foot, and sobbed, 'Let him wait! I won't be married to-day! I won't be married at all, until the Chapel is properly whitened with lime. There's nothing like lime! Nothing but lime will do!'

So saying, she snatched her little hand out of the Earl's, and ran back to her little house as fast as her little feet would carry her.

'Woe is me!' cried the Earl, striking his forehead. 'What shall I do? All the lime in London comes from the Chalk Farm, and for many weeks now the Chalk Farmer refuses to do business. He has taken a vow not to.'

'Why?' asked Tom.

'Nobody knows,' sighed the Earl.

'Then somebody must find out,' said Tom. 'Come along, Jerry!'

'If you don't mind,' said Jerry, 'I'd rather not. I don't feel well.' And doubling his legs under him, he sat down in the Chapel porch.

'It's your own fault if you don't,' said Tom indignantly.

'What's the good of saying that?' asked Jerry 'When a goat feels as unwell as I do now, and is told to come along, and *can't* come along, it doesn't make any difference whose fault it is. Talking won't help. Only time will. You must give me time.'

'I can't give you time,' cried Tom, 'I haven't got any to spare. All the time you waste here feeling sick, Gogmagog is stripping the cherry-trees bare!'

'It is a pity,' said Jerry, 'but I don't see how it can be helped.' And he closed his eyes.

bell swung its clapper, and the Chalk Farmer himself came to the door. He was a middle-sized man with hair and beard like his own thatched roof, a weather-beaten skin, deepset eyes, and clothes which were so ingrained with chalk that there was no guessing what their colour had been when they were made.

'Good-day to ye, brother,' said the Chalk Farmer.

'Same to you, brother,' said the Burly Baker.

'Come in and bite,' said the Chalk Farmer.

At the prospect of a meal Jerry jumped out of the cart like a kid, and Tom also followed readily; but the Burly Baker sat where he was.

'Well, I don't know as there's time,' he said slowly. 'We're in a bit of a hurry, you see.'

'Always time for a snack o' cheese,' insisted the Chalk Farmer, and the Burly Baker got down reluctantly. Tom did not understand his reluctance until he entered the kitchen; then he saw that there was nothing on the table but plates and knives and a dish containing a huge lump of chalk. The Chalk Farmer cut a big wedge for each of his guests and another for himself, which he began to munch with relish. Tom looked in despair at his wedge, until he observed that the Burly Baker was crumbling his to a powder which he pretended to carry to his mouth, and then let fall on the floor. There was already so much chalk on the floor that a little more would never be noticed. Tom was only too glad to follow his example.

'Ah, ah!' said the Chalk Farmer, smacking his lips. 'A rare good cheese be this, this be!' And the Burly Baker smacked his lips, and Tom smacked his. Jerry had crawled in disgust under the table, where he crouched, looking very sulky; he could chew most things, but chalk was one too many for him.

'And now, brother,' said the Chalk Farmer, 'what be ye come about?'

'It's about a matter of lime,' said the Burly Baker. 'Just a cartload will do.'

The Chalk Farmer shook his head. 'It can't be did,' he said.

'That's stuff and nonsense, brother. Your chalk looks as plentiful as ever it did, and where there's chalk there's lime.'

'Ay, ye may say so,' said the Chalk Farmer, 'and I don't deny but I've as fine a crop o' chalk this year as any in England. But before it can be turned into lime it's got to be burned in the kiln; and before it's burned in the kiln, it's got to be hewed out of the quarry. And who's to hew and burn it, that's what I want to know.'

'Who but Clement and Clifford, your own two sons, and my own two nephews, brother?'

'Your nephews if ye like, brother, but no sons

'Whose tea is it?' asked the Burly Baker.

'Never you mind whose tea it is,' said the Maiden. 'I know my place, and I can hold my tongue. Please to state your wants.'

'They're soon stated. Where's my two nephews, Clement and Clifford?'

'Are they expecting you?' asked the Maiden.

'I couldn't say that,' said the Burly Baker.

'Then it's not my place to tell you where they are,' said the Maiden primly. 'Excuse me, please.'

She picked up the tea-tray, and went on stepping neatly down the Lane.

'What shall we do now?' asked Tom.

'Follow her,' said the Burly Baker. 'There was two tea-cups on that tray, and two plates, and two currant loaves, and two pats of butter. My nephews have a weakness for currant bread above all else, and in my opinion that was their tea.'

He got down from the cart, hitched it to a lamp-post, and went after the Maiden, stealthily followed by Tom, Jerry, and Simon. She turned a corner, crossed a road or two, and presently turned another corner which led to a quiet private street where the houses had deep basements, and the windows in the areas were heavily barred. Down one of these the Maiden tripped, and let herself in with a key. As soon as the door was closed,

the Burly Baker went down the steps and rang the area
bell. There was a short pause, and then the Maiden re-
appeared without the tray.

'Yes, sir?' she said, as though she had never seen Tom
and the Baker before.

'Are Clement and Clifford at home, miss?' asked the
Burly Baker.

'I'll go and see,' said the Maiden. She popped into a
door, and popped out again.

'What name, please?'

'I'm John, the young gentlemen's own uncle born,'
said the Burly Baker, 'and this is Tom, a friend of mine,
and this is Jerry his goat, and that is Simon his owl. Now,
miss, are Clem and Cliff at home?'

'I'll go and see,' said the Maiden; and in she popped,
and out again.

'State your business,' said she.

'I don't know as you'd call it business,' said the
Burly Baker. 'We've come friendly like, just to have a
chat with Clem and Cliff – if so be as they're at
home.'

'I'll go and see,' said the Maiden; and in and out she
popped again.

'Are you quite sure you don't come from the Old
Bailey?' she asked.

for their guests, and the two saucers for themselves.

'Well, now, what's it all about?' asked the Burly Baker, when they were comfortably settled, 'and how did it all begin?'

'It began with our love of liming Sparrows,' said Clement.

'If only we could have stopped at Sparrows it mightn't have mattered,' said Clifford. 'Unluckily, one day we heard of other things. Robins and Nightingales,' he whispered.

'Woodpeckers and Starlings!' added Clement.

'Crows and Ringdoves!' said Clifford.

'Cuckoos and Peacocks!' cried Clement.

'And a White Owl!' they shouted together. Then their voices dropped back to a whisper, and they said, 'Hush!' and stared reproachfully at Tom and the Burly Baker, as though they had been making all the noise.

'All these things,' resumed Clifford, 'so we were told, had made their nests in a clump of nine elm-trees a long way off. We thought of them by day, and we dreamed of them by night.'

'We lost all taste for catching Sparrows,' said Clement.

'Even Pigeons palled,' said Clifford.

'One day,' said Clement, 'we could endure it no more. We took a sack of lime, and set out for the Nine

Elms. When we reached them we found that the story was only too true. In every tree a different bird had made its home. We hardly knew where to begin. Think! think of liming a Nightingale, and hearing its song for ever! Think of liming a Robin, and always having a friend in the house! Think of a Cuckoo always to tell us the time by the clock! Think of a Peacock always at hand to spread its beauty before us! Think of a White Owl always there to offer us wisdom—'

'Upon my word!' muttered Simon.

'What's that?' cried Clement, staring at him in amazement. 'Look, Clifford, look! The White Owl!' And his hand began to creep towards his pocket which was stuffed with lime.

'Drop it!' said Simon sharply. 'You can't catch *me* with lime, *or* with chaff. The cheek of you youngsters passes all understanding – as though Wisdom could be won with a handful of dust! Besides, I'm not a White Owl, I'm a brown one, as you'll soon see for yourselves, if the Maiden will brush me down while you tell your tale.'

The Maiden came at once with a feather duster, and set to work dusting Simon, Tom, and Jerry, while Clifford took up the tale where Clement had left it.

'We were soon busy trying to catch the birds, which were treasures such as we'd never thought to own. But unluckily every effort failed; all we did was to startle the birds out of their trees, and the air grew noisy with their cries – the Crow cawed, the Starlings twittered, the Robin piped, the Nightingale trilled, the Ringdove cooed, the Cuckoo cucked, the Owl hooted, the Woodpecker laughed, and the Peacock screamed. So loud it screamed that it brought the Old Bailey down on us, whose job it is to look after the birds. We saw him coming, and took to our heels as the birds took to their wings. All round London he chased us, in and out of every gate, and up and down every street, and as he ran he shouted that he would have the law on us. At last we gave him the slip, and hid ourselves in here, and in we have been ever since, for we dare not go out.'

Then Clifford took a gulp of tea, and Clement a bite of currant bread, and they looked anxiously from Tom to the Burly Baker, and from the Burly Baker back to Tom.

'Well, it *is* a pretty kettle o' fish,' said the Burly Baker, 'and *no* mistake. But perhaps the Old Bailey has quieted down by now.'

'He may have,' said Clement, 'if all his birds have come back. But who's to find out? *We* daren't.'

'But we dare,' said the Burly Baker. 'So we'll just trot along and get it settled, for your father wants you at home to quarry the lime. And a lot depends on your going home soon.'

'We'll do that,' said Clifford earnestly, 'just as soon as the Old Bailey stops having the law on us.'

'There's no time to lose,' said the Burly Baker. 'Good-bye, lads.'

'Good-bye, Uncle.'

'Good-bye, Mr. Clement; good-bye, Mr. Clifford,' said Tom, 'and thank you very much for the nice tea.'

'Good-bye,' said Clement and Clifford. Then each took one of Tom's hands and said, 'Never lime birds if you value your peace.'

'That's the most sensible thing you've said yet,' remarked Simon. 'Mind you live up to it hereafter.'

21

THE OLD BAILEY

IT WAS BEGINNING to be dusk when the Burly Baker unhitched his horse from the lamp-post and set out with Tom for the Nine Elms. To Tom it seemed a very long time since morning, and both he and Jerry were beginning to feel drowsy; as the cart jogged along, Tom's head dropped lower and lower, until it gave a sudden jerk; then he sat upright, blinked for a moment or two, and began to drop his head again. But Simon, who had been sleepy on and off all day, was now very wide awake. He flew low ahead of the cart, giving his long-drawn call; presently from a distance came an answering cry, and out of the twilight a great White Owl flew to meet him. For a moment they seemed to pause together in mid-air, then the White Owl turned and flew back the way it had come, with Simon beside it, and the cart jogging after.

Soon a beautiful trilling song mingled with the calling of the owls, so beautiful that when it began to pierce Tom's dreams he had to wake up to listen. It was a Nightingale singing somewhere to the Evening Star.

Now a group of trees loomed into view; nine tall trunks rose up from the earth and lost themselves in their own leaves. From one of these came the song of the Nightingale, but the bird was too tiny to be seen, though it made the very leaves shake with the beauty of its song.

Under the trees stood the figure of an old man in gaiters and a green coat; he was peering into the sky this way and that, and when he saw the two birds flying towards him he started forward eagerly, crying to the White Owl, 'Solon! Solon! have you brought him home?' Then he looked closer at Simon, sighed impatiently, and muttered, 'Tcha! tcha! it's only another owl, after all.'

'What sort of a bird are you wanting?' asked the Burly Baker, pulling up beside him.

'A Peacock, master,' said the Old Bailey, 'my Peacock, that has disappeared this many a day, ever since two rascally rapscallions came here to lime my birds. They so frightened them that all flew away, and when I got back after chasing those rapscallions in vain, my nine trees were empty. If ever I catch those rapscallions, I'll have the law of them!'

'Oh, don't do that!' begged Tom. 'You've got your Owl back, and your Nightingale.'

'I've got them all back, except my Peacock,' said the Old Bailey. 'When those two rascals had given me the slip, I set my men to watch all the ways to Chalk Farm, in case they should try to sneak home, and then I started hunting London for my birds. But London's a big place, and I was about giving up hope when one day I saw a flock of Duck passing over. They weren't wild duck, but tame duck, and I knew they must come from the Serpentine, where they are born and bred, and grow fat with what the children bring them every day. They bring so much that the Ducks eat what they can, and leave the rest. It surprised me to see them on the wing. So I called out, "Hi! Where are you going, you Ducks?" And the Leader called back, "Where we can get something to eat." "Why," said I, "there's always more to eat in Hyde Park than you and the swans can manage between you." "There was once," said the Leader-Duck, "but we've been eaten out of house and home by a flock of Starlings, that settled there some weeks ago." "Starlings!" said I; "how many of them?" "About a million," said the Leader-Duck, "and a few odd things besides, such as a Cuckoo, a Woodpecker, and a Crow, but they hardly count. It's the Starlings that are starving us, and we're going." "Now don't you be silly," I said, "you know very well that the London children can't do without their Ducks; just you turn round again and lead me to the spot." Well, so they did, sir, and when we got to Hyde Park, there sure enough I found my birds. They'd taken refuge in the Birdcage there, and whenever they were hungry they flew out for the children's crumbs. But when they saw me coming, they crowded into the Cage and shut the door. "Come out o' that!" said I, and Solon, who's their spokesman, said, "No, not a feather of us. We've no mind to be limed by Clement and Clifford. If they catch us, they'll put us in a cage as sure as fate." "And what have you put yourselves in?" said I. "A cage is a cage, whoever shuts the door." At that the birds looked rather silly, and I followed it up with telling them that Clement and Clifford had made themselves scarce, and would be shut up themselves if they showed the tips of their noses again round the Nine Elms. So the birds agreed to come home, and when we got back I saw 'em settled in their own trees – the Robin, the Cuckoo, the Ringdove, the Nightingale, the Crow, the Woodpecker, the White Owl, and the million Starlings.'

'That's only eight kinds,' said Tom, who had been counting on his fingers.

'Yes, young master. My ninth kind, which was the Peacock, was missing, and I don't know where he is. And until I *do* know, Clement and Clifford will do well to lie low, for if ever I catch them I'll have the law of them!'

'But suppose we find your Peacock for you,' said Tom, 'and Clement and Clifford promise never to go liming again, won't you forgive them? I wish you would, because if you don't Gogmagog will eat up Jinny Jones.'

'If that's the hang of it,' said the Old Bailey, 'I'll let Clement and Clifford go home as soon as I've got my Peacock back. But not before, mind ye, not one moment before!'

22

THE OXFORD CIRCUS

'THE NEXT THING,' said Tom to the Burly Baker, as they turned away, 'is to find the Old Bailey's Peacock.'

'It may be *your* next thing,' said the Burly Baker, 'but mine is to go home to bed. I'll drive you a bit of the way, and put you down anywhere you fancy.'

'I don't fancy anywhere but where the Peacock is,' said Tom.

'And that's a matter of luck,' said the Burly Baker, 'so we may as well jog along towards Baker Street and take our chances.'

Tom could offer no better advice, and the cart was soon rattling merrily on its way.

Within a mile of Baker Street it had to pull up and go slow for the road was crowded with a stream of children, moving eagerly in one direction. Every child held a new penny in its hand, and all were chattering excitedly, but what they were saying was so mixed up that Tom could only hear a word here and there. The words were all nice ones, however, and full of promise:

such as 'Elephants!' and 'Clowns!' and 'Paper Hoops!'

Tom leaned over the side of the cart and called, 'Where are you going?'

The boy nearest to him looked up and answered, 'To the Circus. It's a prime one, they say, travelled all the way from Oxford. You'd better come too. It's only a penny.'

'Oh, dear,' said Tom, 'I would like to. But I haven't time – and I haven't a penny.'

'What a pity,' said the boy. 'There's a lot of good things in it, but the best of all, they say, is Jack the Juggler. He's the King of Jugglers, they say. I wouldn't miss seeing *him*, not for Twopence!'

'Oh, dear,' said Tom, 'so wouldn't I if I had it – and if I wasn't going somewhere else.'

'Where else are you going?' asked the boy.

'I don't quite know,' said Tom.

'Then you might as well go to the Circus as anywhere,' said the boy.

'Well,' said Tom doubtfully, 'perhaps I might – if I had a penny.'

'I'll stand you the penny,' said the Burly Baker.

The Oxford Circus was now in sight. Tom saw a big dark blue tent in the middle of an open place where several roads met; along all the roads children streamed, and their bright faces were lit up by the ring of flaring lights around the tent. There was sawdust strewn all around for yards outside, orange-sellers and sweetstuff-sellers were walking about with their trays of good things, and an Oxford Don stood at the flap of the tent playing ten musical instruments at once. Near him a Senior Wrangler with a red nose and wide pink trousers was banging on a drum, and calling, 'One Penny! Only One Penny! Ponies and Elephants and Performing Dogs! Bareback Riders and Trapeze Flyers and Tumbling Clowns! All for One Penny, only One Penny! Pay up, pay up, pay up!'

It was all so exciting that Tom had to think very hard indeed about Jinny Jones; and he had almost thought hard enough, when he caught sight of the long Circus Poster hanging on the tent. In the middle it said, in big coloured letters:

STAR TURN!
JACK THE JUGGLER!

and underneath was a marvellous picture of a queer man, juggling with the stars, the sun, and the moon. This was altogether too much for Tom, and he whispered longingly to Simon,

'Simon! what do you think?'

'Take the boy's advice,' said Simon. 'If you're to stop anywhere, why not here? And if here, why stop outside, when inside is better?'

Tom turned to the Burly Baker and said, 'Well, sir, if you really can spare a penny.'

And the Burly Baker said, 'Boys will be boys,' and gave him the penny, and drove away.

Tom took his place in the queue of children, and shuffled along with the rest; but when his turn came to pay up, the Oxford Don looked hard at Jerry and Simon and said, 'No Counter-Attractions admitted. All birds and animals to be left outside in the Pen.'

'Oh dear!' said Tom. 'I hope it's a nice Pen?'

'It's supposed to be the best Pen in the College,' said the Don, and turning to a young Freshman he ordered, 'Here, take these creatures and lock them up behind the Newdigate.'

'Suppose they escape?' said Tom anxiously. 'They're awfully good at getting through things.'

'Scarcely anybody gets through the Newdigate,' said the Don, 'and if they do, they have to carry it about with them for the rest of their lives.'

'How dreadful,' said Tom.

'It is rather,' said the Don. He waved the creatures away, bit Tom's penny, nodded approvingly, and said, 'Pass, with Honours!'

Tom passed into the tent, and got a seat on the very front bench, behind the red rope that ran all round the Ring. He hadn't any money for a programme, so he didn't know when Jack the Juggler's turn would come, but what with the Band and the Clowns and the Horses and the Ladies flying through Paper Hoops and Wreaths of Roses, and Balliol the Ring-Master cracking his whip, and a Comic Donkey, and a Pink-and-Silver Man on a Tight-Rope in the air, and a Blue-and-Gold Girl on a Ball on the ground, he was content to wait till the fellow came who could play with the Stars and the Sun and the Moon. Presently he saw everybody rustling their red and green programmes excitedly, and he knew in his bones that Jack was coming next.

A buzz went round the tent, and everybody watched expectantly the opening through which the performers came in and out. But instead of Jack, Ring-Master Balliol appeared, and walking to the middle of the Ring he held up his hand for silence. Then he said:

'I regret to say that Jack the Juggler will not appear to-night!'

Instead of a buzz, a tremendous groan now went round the tent.

'Yes, I know,' said the Master. 'I'm very sorry. But the truth is he disappeared some time ago, and we don't know where he is.'

'Shame!' cried several people at once. 'You ought to have the bills altered, then!'

'Yes, I know,' said the Master. 'Meanwhile, in Jack's

place we have a Super-Attraction to offer, a Marvellous Illusion which we call The Birth of the Peacock Butterfly.'

This sounded promising, and the discontent died down a little. The Master cracked his whip, and in ran a troop of children, in gleaming butterfly dresses of blue and green and gold, bearing on their uplifted hands an immense egg of the same colours. This they set on end in the middle of the tent; the Master cracked it with his whip, and it fell apart in two pieces. Inside was a great cocoon of glittering coloured silk. Now every child took an end of one of the silken strands, and running out to the barrier of red rope stood in a ring all round the Circus. At another crack of the Master's whip the Band began to play the most airy fairy music, while the children ran swiftly round and round the ring, holding the silken threads as in a Maypole Dance. As they ran the cocoon unwound itself, and the air was filled with shimmering floss, blue, rose and gold, green, yellow and silver, while the audience gazed at the dwindling cocoon through a whirling rainbow of silken light. Presently the last strand was unwound, the children stood still letting the shining threads float downwards, and a strange folded object was revealed poised upright on a golden lily-cup. The music increased in loveliness, and very slowly the object unfolded itself. A crest sprang up on its head, a gleaming neck and body were displayed, and feather by feather, as it seemed, a glittering arc sprang up behind the head and body, spreading until it seemed to fill the tent. The music grew faster, the Butterfly-Bird began to twirl round and round on the lily so that every one in the Circus could see and admire it, the tent was crowded with the glitter and rattle of its marvellous feathers. Suddenly the top of the tent opened, the Butterfly-Bird rose up on its wings, and with tail full-spread sailed up into the sky like a rocket, and disappeared.

The Audience screamed and clapped with joy – all except Tom, who had sat breathless through the wonderful transformation scene. But when the tent-top closed, he scrambled under the rope, rushed up to the Master, clutched his gown, and cried,

'Give me that Peacock!'

'Bless my soul!' said the Master.

'Give me that Peacock!' repeated Tom, shaking him fiercely. 'He isn't yours!'

'Hush!' said the Master. 'Come outside.'

He hurried Tom outside before the astonished audience had time to realise what was happening, and the Circus went on without him.

23

JACK'S STRAW CASTLE

'EXPLAIN YOURSELF, IF you please!' said the Master, when he had got Tom outside to himself.

He looked very imposing, but not unkind; Tom told him everything in one breath, and ended, 'So if the Old Bailey doesn't get his Peacock back, Gogmagog will eat up Jinny Jones, and please, sir, isn't your Peacock the Old Bailey's Peacock, for I really think it must be.'

'Now that you put it like that,' said the Master thoughtfully, 'I think so too. But it's a rare Predicament.'

'Is Predicament Oxford for Peacock, sir?' asked Tom.

'Sometimes,' said the Master thoughtfully. 'As now. You see, my boy, when Jack the Juggler ran away, nobody knows where or why, it sent the Circus down at once. It's a bad thing to happen in any case, but in Oxford to be Sent Down is the worst thing that can happen. Well, one day I was walking in the High, wondering what on earth we should do to get Sent Up again. The High happened to be unusually full of Blues—'

'What are Blues?' asked Tom.

'The Best and Brightest and most Beautiful of creatures,' said the Master; 'yet that day I noticed that among them was one still Better, Brighter, and more Beautiful than the rest – and even Bluer. It was the Peacock. Where he had come from it did not occur to me to wonder. He seemed quite natural there among the others. What I did see was that he could be turned into a Super-Attraction for the Circus, to take Jack's place. We needed so badly to regain our Prestige.'

'Is Prestige Oxford for Peacock too?' asked Tom.

'Frequently,' admitted the Master. 'Well, there it is, you see.'

'Yes, sir,' said Tom. 'And can I have it, please?'

'Certainly!' said the Master; 'certainly! As soon as you have found Jack the Juggler, and induced him to return to us, you shall have the Peacock to do with what you will.'

'Oh, sir—' cried Tom appealingly.

'No thanks, my boy, no thanks,' said the Master. 'Justice is justice. The bird shall be yours. And now I must return to the Ring.'

And patting Tom's head kindly, he disappeared through the flap of the tent.

Tom sat down where he was, and put his hands very tight over his mouth to keep back his disappointment.

'What's the matter now?' hooted Simon's familiar voice in his ear.

Tom winked hard, and said, 'Oh, Simon, I've found the Peacock, but now I've got to find Jack, and my legs are so tired. How did you get out of the Pen?'

'Jerry carried off the Newdigate on his head,' said Simon. 'There he comes now.'

Tom saw Jerry ambling up; his beard was full of straw from the Pen, and on his horns the Newdigate was impaled.

'See what I've done?' boasted Jerry.

'More fool you!' said Simon. 'There's a thing to saddle yourself with.'

'Why shouldn't he be saddled to it?' said Tom suddenly. 'Then I can ride on it, like a sleigh.'

'Here I say!' said Jerry; but Tom took no notice. He unhooked the Newdigate from Jerry's horns, laid it on the ground behind him, and hitched it to him with a length of string from his pocket. Then he seated himself upon it, gripped the two sides, and cried, 'Off you go!'

'Which way?' grumbled Jerry.

'As the straws blow in the wind,' said Simon. 'Follow your beard, Jerry, and you'll get there.'

Jerry ran his eye down his nose, saw the straws blow north, and north he went.

It had long been night, and a dark one. Tom looked

in vain for stars to guide them, and as they sped up the northern heights hugged himself to keep the wind out of his bones. Presently they seemed to have come to the top. Before them lay a great round pond, with a little tail to it like a comet, and though the sky was black, the pond sparkled with light. Jerry ran to the edge and peered in, and Tom jumped off the gate, and peered in too. The still cold water was crowded with stars, which were strewn and piled on its bed like shells and pebbles at the bottom of the sea.

'How lovely they are!' said Tom. 'However did they get there?'

'Fell out of the sky, of course,' said Jerry. 'Don't you see there are none left up there?'

'Yes, I suppose so,' said Tom. 'Where are we going now?'

'Nowhere!' said Jerry decidedly. 'The wind's stopped blowing.'

'I wish it had stopped where there was some sort of shelter,' said Tom, shivering.

'Are you cold?' asked a voice behind him.

Tom turned, and saw a lean, supple young man, with wisps of fair hair hanging about his brows and cheekbones. He had a simple face, and pale blue eyes that seemed to be asking a sort of question, and a long thin mouth where a vague smile wandered.

'Yes, I'm *very* cold,' said Tom.

'Come to my Castle, then,' said the simple young man.

'Have you got a real Castle?' asked Tom.

The young man nodded. 'I built it all by myself,' he said. 'It isn't *quite* finished. But I think I could finish it if your goat would come too.'

'I'm no builder,' said Jerry cautiously. 'Everybody knows that. I'm famed for not being. So don't you go putting me to build for you.'

'Oh, I don't want you to do any work,' said the simple young man. 'I only want to weed the straws out of your beard and coat. Then I can finish the south wall.'

'With straw?' said Tom.

'Of course,' said Jerry importantly. 'You can't make bricks without straw. Even *I* know that.'

'Oh, I don't make bricks at all,' said the young man. 'I just use the straw as it is. It's so much quicker. And it's very nice, except in a high wind, and very warm too. Come along.'

They followed him for a few yards across the road, and found themselves before a queer crazy building made of straw, with walls of cornstalk, a roof like a haycock, and no windows at all. The ground outside was littered with stubble, and a small opening had been left to creep through.

'This is my Castle,' said the simple young man, in a happy voice; and he said again, 'I built it all myself. Will you come in, Mr. Goat, and Mr. Owl, and – I don't know your name.'

'My name is Tom,' said Tom.

'Mine,' said the simple young man, 'is Jack.'

'Jack!' cried Tom excitedly.

'Yes. Jack. Jack Straw. Will you come in, Tom? There's something so pretty inside.'

24

THE ANGEL

THE GROUND INSIDE Jack Straw's Castle was even deeper in straw than the outside. Tom's feet sank in the warm gold litter up to the ankles. The little room was round like a beehive, and ran up to a high conical point. Tom had expected it to be dark, but in the very top of the cone hung a star, and here and there clusters of other stars clung like bees about the walls. At the back of the room was a big heap of straw like a couch, or a half-made haystack, and something was lying on, or rather in it. Jack put his finger to his lips and beckoned Tom to follow him. They tiptoed across, and Jack pulled away a little of the straw so that Tom could peep.

'Here's my pretty thing,' said Jack.

Jack's pretty thing was nothing more nor less than an Angel. She wasn't a very big one, but she was quite complete. Her wings were folded round her, so that all you saw was her little gold head coming out of the feathers.

While they looked at her she stirred, and opened her

eyes, which were as blue as the sky. Seeing Tom she sat up and said 'Goot efening!' to him in the sweetest tones he had ever heard.

'Good-evening,' said Tom.

'Then you've found a new friend, look you, Jack,' said the Angel.

'I've found three,' said Jack delightedly. 'A boy and a bird and a beast. This one's the boy. That's the bird flown up to sit in the star in the roof. And the one over there is the beast.' He pointed to Jerry, who had settled down, and was munching a hole in the wall.

'Oh dear!' said Tom. 'He's eating you out of house and home.'

'So he is,' said Jack. 'I expect he's hungry, poor thing. We can soon mend it, you know.' He sat down by the Angel, and motioned to Tom to sit too. 'Did you have a sweet dream?' he asked her.

'Yes, Jack, I thank you kindly. I dreamed I found my Harp whatever.'

'She's lost her Harp,' said Jack rather sadly to Tom.

'What sort of Harp?' asked Tom.

'A Welsh one. She's a Welsh Angel, you see. One day the Circus I used to be with travelled to Wales. That's where I saw and heard her. She was sitting among the children, and while I was juggling with the stars I knew for the first time that all my life I had only practised with them to give her pleasure. You know, Tom, I'd played with the stars from my cradle, and when I threw them up in the air and made patterns with them, or caused them to sing sweetly one against the other, there was always something lovely I wanted to see them do, and hear them sing, that I couldn't quite see and hear. But when I saw the Angel among the children all my stars made the right patterns and sang the very music. So after the Circus was over and the people went out, I went out after her. Yes, I went after her all the way to Islington.'

'Is this Islington?' asked Tom.

Jack shook his head. 'They kept her there for a bit, but after a while they turned her out,' he said. 'It's funny to have an Angel and turn it out, isn't it? I expect they didn't really know. So I drowned most of my stars in the pond outside, and built her a Castle here, for us to stay in for ever, even when she is better.'

'Is she ill?' asked Tom.

'Her wing is hurt. While she was flying from Islington, some one shot at her, and broke one of her feathers. She managed to flutter here, only what with shock, you know, she dropped her Harp, and that is how she came to lose it. But her wing is mending nicely.'

'When you left,' said Tom, 'it sent the Circus down.'

'Did it?' said Jack. 'Now why, I wonder.'

'Because you were the Star Turn.'

'Was I?' said Jack. 'How funny.'

'Didn't you know?' said Tom.

'I don't remember,' said Jack. He felt in his pocket, took out a handful of stars, and began to toss them in the air. The straw room suddenly became full of beauty and sweet sounds, and the stars on the walls began to tremble and move in changing patterns up and down, like silver bees on a honeycomb.

'Oh, Jack!' cried Tom, when the performance ended. 'Won't you go back to the Circus?'

'No,' said Jack joyfully, 'never no more.'

'Your little boy friend is going to cry, look you,' said the Angel, stroking Tom's head.

Jack looked very sad again. 'I wonder why, now,' he said.

Then Tom began his tale, and told him. At the end he said, 'You wouldn't like Gogmagog to eat Jinny Jones, would you, Jack?'

'No,' said Jack. He stuffed the stars into his pocket. 'Well then, Tom, I'll go back to the Circus. But my Angel must come with me, to play for me while I juggle. You can't do without your Angel, once you've found it.'

'You will go with him, won't you?' begged Tom, 'and play for him as he wants you to.'

'Oh dear, oh dear, I must find my Harp first, look you,' pleaded the Angel. 'I cannot play on anything but my Harp.'

'Will you find her Harp for her?' asked Jack. 'I've looked for it everywhere, high and low, and in and out, and I *can't* find it.'

'All right, I'll try,' said Tom bravely. 'Good-night, Jack. Good-night, Angel. Come on, Jerry. Come on, Simon.'

And they stepped all three into the night again.

25

THE SWISS COTTAGE

WHEN TOM LEFT Jack's Castle, he asked nobody's advice which way to go. He was too tired to think, and just let his legs tumble where they would. And as things that tumble always tumble down, down hill they tumbled.

They had hardly tumbled a mile when they heard a sort of singing, like somebody practising. Whoever it was had a very hoarse voice, and the words of the song were like nothing Tom had ever heard before. The words were:

'*Li-ee-li-ee-liee-eu!*'

over and over and over again.

'What a funny language,' said Tom. 'I wonder what it is.'

'*I* can tell you,' said Jerry. 'I mayn't know much, but I do know that. Any goat does. That is the Swiss Language, and there isn't any more of it. That's all there is of it from A to Z.'

'What does it mean?' asked Tom.

'Whatever you like, as long as it's happy,' said Jerry.
'Such as: "How bright the sun shines on the snow!" or
"How pretty little Liesel in the valley is!" or "How
clever I was to get to the top!" or "Oh, how I do like
Gruyère cheese!" All happy things like that, see?'

'It doesn't sound very happy *now*,' said Tom. And it
certainly didn't, for the Singer's voice croaked like a
crow at the bottom, and cracked like a cup at the top.

As they got nearer they heard him complaining in
between his attempts to sing.

'*Ach Himmel! O Ciel!*' said he. 'Mine voice is gone
away for good and all. Will I never get back mine
beautiful voice? Ohé!'

And then he began to practise again his '*Li-ee-li-ee-
liee-eu!*' But on the last '*Liee!*' his voice cracked worse
than ever.

Tom turned a corner, and the Singer came into
sight. He was a stalwart young Swiss in a green cap with
a feather in it, and he was seated outside a charming
little cottage of brown wood, covered with little carved
balconies and outside staircases; the balconies and
staircases were crowded with pots of blooming flowers;
the edge of the roof was like fretwork, and on the top it
was held down by big stones set here and there upon it.
Against the wall, by the side of the young man, leaned a
long staff with a metal point, and a bow and arrows

stood there too. In his hand he held an immense slice of yellow soap with holes in it, from which every now and then he comforted himself with a bite.

Seeing three strangers approach, he sprang up, shaded his eyes with his hand, and then, swiftly fitting an arrow to his bow, he pointed it at Simon.

'Stop!' cried Tom.

'*Pourquoi?*' asked the Swiss.

'Because that's my Owl,' said Tom.

'*Verzeihung!*' said the Swiss. 'I thought it was the Golden Eagle of the Jungfrau.' And he turned his arrow on Jerry instead.

'Stop!' cried Tom again.

'*Warum?*' inquired the Swiss.

'Because that's my Goat,' said Tom.

'*Excusez!*' said the Swiss. 'I took him for the Silver Chamois of Mont Blanc.' He put away his bow and added, 'Welcome all! Have some cheese.'

'No, thank you,' said Tom, who had already sampled cheese once lately, and thought that soap would be no pleasanter than chalk.

'More fool you!' said Jerry, taking a huge bite. 'Goat's milk cheese is the best in the world.'

Tom whispered to Simon, 'Is it really cheese?'

Simon nodded, and Tom took a bit, and found that it wasn't at all like soap, and much more like wild strawberries. So they all sat down and munched contentedly, while the Swiss asked,

'Did you hear me singing as you came along?'

'We couldn't help it,' said Tom.

'No doubt. I have the strongest Yodel in London. But what,' he added anxiously, 'did you really think of it?'

'Do you really mean really?' asked Tom.

'Yes, really.'

'It hurt my ears,' said Tom.

The Swiss nodded sadly. 'I feared so. It hurt my throat.'

'Then why did you do it?' asked Tom.

'It is like this,' said the Swiss. 'I am Yodeller to King Lud of London, and of all the sounds that soothe his soul, my Yodel soothes it best. Now King Lud – By the way,' he broke off, 'do you know King Lud?'

'No,' said Tom. 'I know almost everybody else, but not him.'

'Well,' resumed the Swiss, 'if you knew him, I need not explain that King Lud is a King of Many Moods. In one moment he is in one mood, and in the next in another. In the morning he is bright, in the evening he is foggy. Now he is as boisterous as the wind, and then he is as black as the chimney-smoke. There's no counting on him at all. He is as changeable as the

London weather. Well, you must know he is passionately fond of cherries when they are in season.'

'Yes, yes!' cried Tom. 'I know he is!'

'And when he is disappointed of his cherries, he grows as cross as two sticks.'

'Yes, yes!' cried Tom. 'I know he does!'

'And when he is as cross as two sticks,' said the Swiss, 'there's no telling *what* he'll do.'

'Yes, there is!' cried Tom. 'He'll throw his sceptre into the Thames.'

'*Mille Tonnerres* and *Donnerwetter!*' exclaimed the Swiss. 'You know it then!'

'I heard the King's Cook tell the King's Cherry-Seller,' said Tom.

'Then know further,' said the Swiss, 'that the moment he lost his sceptre he regretted it. Its loss so disturbs him that he cannot sleep unless his soul is soothed. To my lot fell it to soothe him with my Yodel day and night; but having to Yodel for twenty-four hours on end is bad for even the strongest voice. After doing it, I have lost mine entirely, and what I sing soothes him no more.'

'What does, then?' asked Tom.

'Fortunately,' said the Swiss, 'I am good at musical instruments too, and I happen to have a very nice one in my cottage there. So I play it for him instead, and meanwhile practise gently at my voice, trying to coax it back. For I am sorry to say King Lud does not like my harp as well as he likes my voice.'

'Your harp?' said Tom quickly.

'Yes. Would you like to hear me play it?' The Swiss reached his hand behind the cottage door, and produced a beautiful little harp of gold. The three sides of it were carved like three leeks, and at the top corner, peeping from the long flag-like leaves, was a lovely little head, exactly like the Angel's in Jack Straw's Castle.

'Oh, oh!' cried Tom excitedly. 'Where did you get that harp?'

'It was by great good luck,' said the Swiss. 'Some while ago, when I was out hunting, I saw high in the air a white and golden bird flying in the sun. I had never seen the like before. I aimed my arrow and shot, and fancied I had winged it; nevertheless, it fluttered on and escaped. But in passing it dropped this harp, which I have cherished ever since.'

'It is the very harp I am looking for,' said Tom earnestly. And once more he related his story, and ended as usual, 'So if you do not give me the harp, Gogmagog will eat up Jinny Jones as soon as he has finished the cherry trees. And then she'll be dead.'

'But so, if I give you the harp, will I be,' observed the Swiss. 'For if I can neither sing nor play to King Lud, he will have my head cut off in one moment, and be sorry for it in the next. But that won't help me then. If I hadn't lost my voice, it wouldn't matter.'

Tom scratched his head. 'I've been asked to find a lot of things since yesterday morning,' he said, 'but I don't see how I can find your lost voice.'

'I can find that for myself,' said the Swiss, 'when I can have a fortnight's holiday to rest it in. But suppose now you were to find King Lud's sceptre itself. Then he wouldn't want me to soothe him, and I could give you the harp. That would solve everything.'

'So it would!' cried Tom hopefully. 'What part of the Thames did he throw his sceptre in?'

'That I don't know,' said the Swiss, 'for I wasn't there.'

'Then I'll go and ask him. Come, Simon! come, Jerry!' And out into the dawn ran Tom once more, as fast as his heels could carry him.

26

KING LUD

THE PALACE OF King Lud was the easiest place in all London to find. Everybody Tom met and asked knew it, Policemen, Postmen, Cabmen, Road Sweepers, Soldiers, Sailors, Nursemaids, and all. So he ran straight to it without once losing his way, and his heart was full of hope, but his stomach was full of emptiness. It was astonishing how empty his stomach was. He mentioned it as he ran, and Jerry said,

'Of course it is. So's mine. We never had our breakfast yesterday.'

'But we had afternoon tea, and sacks of sugar, and cheese, and – and chalk and things, since then,' said Tom.

'We never had our *breakfast*,' repeated Jerry obstinately, 'and if you miss your breakfast, you *miss* your breakfast. To-day we shall need twice as much breakfast as usual, and even more.'

'Have you ever had as much breakfast as you could eat, Jerry?' asked Tom.

'Never,' said Jerry. 'I live for the day.'

'Then you won't have to live long,' hooted Simon.

'Why?' asked Tom.

But all Simon said was, 'Here's the Palace.'

At the Palace Gate stood a Guardsman, six foot high. On seeing Tom, he presented his bayonet and cried:

'Give the Password!'

'Bother!' said Tom.

'Pass!' cried the Guard, and Tom ran like lightning into the Palace grounds, fearing that the Guard would discover his mistake.

In the Palace Porch stood a second Guardsman, seven foot high. He too presented his bayonet, and shouted:

'Give the Password!'

'Bother, *bother!*' said Tom.

'Pass!' shouted the Guard. And on ran Tom till he came to the Throne-Room. At the door stood a third Guardsman, eight foot high; who, presenting his bayonet, roared at Tom once more:

'Give the Password!'

'Bother, *bother*, BOTHER!' exclaimed Tom.

'Pass!' roared the Guardsman; and he threw open the doors of the Throne-Room, and Tom, Jerry, and Simon marched in.

The Throne-Room was full of courtiers, all in a state of the trembles; and at the end, on his golden throne, sat

King Lud, tearing his hair, tearing his purple clothes, tearing the crimson hangings round about him, and crying all the time as he did so:

'Oh, bother! What shall I do? Oh, bother, *bother!* What*ever* shall I do? Oh, bother, *bother*, BOTHER!'

He said it so often, that by the time Tom had crossed the room he had got tired of it. So when he reached the throne he stamped his foot at King Lud and cried, 'What's the use of saying Bother? Stop it at once!'

King Lud stopped it at once, and said in a surprised voice, 'True. What's the use of saying Bother?'

'It doesn't help,' said Tom.

'Not a bit,' said King Lud.

'Then don't do it,' said Tom.

'Then I won't,' said King Lud. 'But – but – but—' And he looked at Tom, and his lower lip trembled. 'But I want my Sceptre, *and I want my Cherries!*' And he burst into tears.

'Stop it!' cried Tom; and King Lud stopped it.

'Don't be cross with me,' he begged, so meekly that Tom began to feel sorry for him, and explained,

'I only said it like that for your good. I want you to have your Sceptre and your Cherries as much as you do.'

'Do you really?' asked King Lud. He turned to his Chamberlain and said in an undertone, 'Put this boy down in the next Birthday Honours List.'

'Yes, I do,' said Tom. 'And once you get your Sceptre, you'll get your Cherries too.' Then for the last time he explained about Gogmagog and Jinny Jones, and ended, 'So if you'll tell me exactly where you threw your Sceptre into the Thames, I'll get it out for you.'

'I'll show you the very spot!' cried King Lud. 'Come along with me.'

And out of the Palace trooped King Lud and Tom Tiddler hand in hand, with Jerry and Simon behind them, and all the Courtiers bringing up the rear.

27

THE BATTER SEA

KING LUD AND his Court marched south and west through London Town, and as they marched the people turned out to see them, and joined the procession. They didn't know what it was about, but that didn't matter, for the People of London Town loved being one of a crowd, wherever it was, for any reason, or for no reason at all. In this way they collected servant-maids and shop-keepers, errand-boys and organ-grinders, clerks and flower-sellers, and all the other sorts of folk you may meet with in your morning stroll. There was a chimney-sweep or two, and a Scotsman with his bagpipes, and a chair-mender, and a scissors-grinder; but more than any other sort there were the children, poor children and rich, all on their way to school But when they saw King Lud's procession they forgot about school, and joined up, tossing their satchels and beating their slates with their pencils.

South they marched till they reached the River, and west they marched to Battersea Bridge. King Lud marched to the very middle of the Bridge, and there he stopped and waved his hand.

'Here it was,' he announced to Tom in a loud voice, so that all could hear, 'that I threw my Sceptre into the Thames in a fit of the tantrums, because there weren't any cherries to be bought in the market.'

'All right,' said Tom, and began to strip off his jacket.

'What are you doing that for?' asked King Lud.

'I'm going to dive for it,' said Tom.

'Think twice about it,' said King Lud; and when Tom had mounted the parapet and gazed down into the Thames below him, he did think twice about it. For there he saw, not a running river, but a great sea of thick yellow batter. Far away down one reach of the Thames he saw Wandsworth Bridge standing with its feet in real water, and far away up the other reach he saw Albert Bridge, with its feet in the water too. But in between, spreading half-way on either hand, it was nothing but batter, stretching from bank to bank, and as to how deep it went down it was impossible to guess. And hidden somewhere in that thick yellow sea lay King Lud's Sceptre. Tom's heart sank as he looked at it.

'Oh, goodness!' said Tom. '*Batter!*'

'Did you say Batter?' said Jerry, and clambered on to the parapet beside him; and when he saw what lay below him, he bleated joyfully, 'Batter! batter! Goodness, indeed!'

He leaped down from the parapet, and started along the Bridge.

'Where are you going?' cried Tom.

'To have my breakfast,' answered Jerry. 'Thistles are better, but batter will do.'

In another moment he was on the river bank, gulping down batter for all he was worth. Tom stared at him, and suddenly felt the empty hole in his own stomach.

'It's all right, King Lud!' he cried. '*We'll* find your Sceptre for you. Simon, fetch me a spoon. I'll help too!' And off he ran to join Jerry on the bank.

Then pandemonium broke out among the schoolboys.

'*We'll help! We'll help!*' they shouted. 'Fetch us all spoons!' And they ran in their thousands, and lined up on either side of the Thames, as far as the sea of batter reached. The Courtiers hurried to buy all the spoons in the neighbouring spoon-shops, and soon every child was provided – some with teaspoons, some with tablespoons, some with egg-spoons, others with salt-spoons; and Tom had a soup ladle. Only Jerry hadn't a spoon, and didn't need one. With his beard dripping batter he was doing more work in one minute than twenty children in ten.

Then how they all set to! You'd have thought to see them that *none* of them had had breakfast since yesterday morning, and perhaps some of them hadn't. Spoonful after spoonful of the thick rich batter they sucked down, while the Crowd on the bridge cheered them on. Presently a small fat boy laid down his spoon, and sighed heavily. But Jerry gobbled on.

'Stick to it, lad!' cried the Crowd.

'I can't,' said the small fat boy. 'I'm as tight as I'll go.'

He was cheered again, for he had had a very good innings, and a Crowd is always the first to appreciate that. Now one by one the children began to lay down their spoons. But Jerry gobbled on.

The Crowd began to make bets as to which would last longest. Tom was a favourite, but the odds were in Jerry's favour. And there were side bets also: would Chelsea Charlie eat more than Bermondsey Bill? Which would outlast the other, Westminster Willie, or Kensington Ken? Would Pimlico Peter or Bertie of Barnes burst first?

Lower and lower sank the Batter Sea, but faster and faster the children dropped out; and still the Sceptre was not in sight. And Jerry gobbled on.

The last of the School children laid down his spoon. And Jerry gobbled on.

Tom was now going slower than when he began.

He kept an anxious eye on the Batter Sea, and the Crowd kept an anxious eye on him. And Jerry gobbled on.

Tom felt his face getting hot. He mopped his brow. Jerry gobbled on.

Tom felt his jacket getting tight. He took it off. Jerry gobbled on.

Tom struggled with every ladleful he now brought out. The Crowd hung on his every mouthful. Jerry gobbled on.

At last came the ladleful that was Tom's finish. With a tremendous effort he got it down, and then he dropped the ladle and rolled over on his face. The Crowd groaned. There was no sign of the Sceptre.

But Jerry gobbled on.

He gobbled till Half-past Twelve, when it was time for the children to come out of school.

He gobbled till Two, when it was time for them to go back.

He gobbled till Four, when it was time for tea.

He gobbled till Six, when it was time for supper.

He gobbled till Seven, when it was time for bed.

And just as Big Ben was booming Seven o'clock from his high tower, Jerry gulped down the last mouthful of the Batter Sea.

Then he cocked one yellow eye towards Chelsea,

and he cocked the other yellow eye towards Wandsworth, and, seeing the Battersea Reach licked high and dry, with not another drop to sup, he said,

'I've done my breakfast. I've had as much as I can eat. I have seen the day.' And he shut his eyes and sat down.

'But where,' cried King Lud, '*where is my Sceptre?*'

'Oh!' said Tom desperately, 'don't say we've done it for nothing!' But up and down the empty river-bed though they searched, not a vestige of the Sceptre was to be seen.

Suddenly Jerry was observed to be writhing on the ground. He lay on his back, kicking his hoofs in the air; he twisted his neck from side to side, and choked and spluttered as though his end had come.

'Jerry! what's the matter with you?' cried Tom, running to him in alarm.

'Bone in my throat!' choked Jerry. 'Must have swallowed a fish. Eee-au! I'm dying!'

'Open your mouth, silly,' commanded Tom, 'and don't kick!'

Jerry opened his mouth, and Tom thrust in his hand. Something long and hard was lodged in Jerry's throat. With a pull, Tom brought it forth to the light.

It was King Lud's Sceptre.

28

AND SO—

AND SO—

Tom Tiddler gave King Lud his Sceptre.

So King Lud gave the Swiss Yodeller's a fortnight's holiday.

So the Swiss Yodeller gave the Angel back her Harp.

So the Angel promised to play it for Jack as long as he juggled for the children.

So Jack the Juggler went back to the Oxford Circus.

So the Oxford Circus-Master restored the Peacock to the Old Bailey.

So the Old Bailey forgave Clement and Clifford for frightening it away.

So Clement and Clifford went back to the Chalk Farm to quarry the lime.

So the Chalk Farmer sent the Earl the lime to whiten the Chapel.

So the Earl and the Lady of Limehouse were married in the Whitechapel, with the Spaniard for their Best Man.

So after the wedding the Spaniard sent his sword to the Old Lady of Threadneedle Street, to make needles of.

So the Old Lady mended the Petticoat for Wormwood.

So Wormwood gave it back to the King's Laundress.

So the King's Laundress hung it up to air in Petticoat Lane, and returned it to the Lass of Lavender Hill.

So the Lavender Lass put it on and went back to the Shepherd's Bush.

So the Shepherd restored the Smith his Hound.

So the Smith made the key for the Leaden Hall, and gave it to Tom Tiddler.

And so—

Tom Tiddler took the key and unlocked the Leaden Hall, all ready for Gogmagog. And then he ran with all his might and main to the Cherry Gardens, to see if Gogmagog had eaten all the cherries yet, and if Jinny Jones and the little girls were still alive.

29

THE CHERRY GARDENS

YOU CAN PICTURE Tom's joy and relief when he reached the Cherry Gardens, and saw Jinny Jones with her face pressed against the gate, watching for him. Behind her were crowded all the other little girls.

'Hurray!' cried Tom. 'Are you all here?'

'Yes,' said Jinny, 'we're all here, Tom. But, oh, Tom! there's only one cherry-tree left with cherries on it. Gogmagog is sleeping after his last meal; when he wakes he'll go to that cherry-tree and eat it up; and after that, if you can't save us, he'll begin on us!'

'*I'll* save you!' said Tom.

'How?' said Jinny Jones.

'I don't know,' said Tom. 'But I've got the key of the Leaden Hall.'

'Yes,' bleated Jerry, 'and that's all *my* doing, that is! If Gogmagog is locked up in the Leaden Hall, it's me you'll have to thank for it.'

'Thank you now, Jerry,' said Jinny Jones.

'Hu-uuh!' hooted Simon. 'Gogmagog isn't in the

Leaden Hall yet. As Jerry's so clever, perhaps he'll tell us how to get Gogmagog there.'

'Perhaps he will,' said Jerry, 'and perhaps he won't. I've done *my* bit, Simon. Suppose you do yours.'

'Oh, Simon,' pleaded Tom, 'do do your bit, and tell me how to get Gogmagog into the Leaden Hall. For I can't even get into the Cherry Gardens to get Jinny Jones out.'

'And if you did,' said Jinny Jones, 'it would be no use. Gogmagog would come after us and catch us again. No, we'll only be safe when he's locked up in the Leaden Hall.'

'Please, Simon,' begged Tom.

'Well, I suppose I must,' said Simon, 'if it's only to stop Jerry thinking he's done it all by finding King Lud's sceptre. And as far as I can see, he did his best to lose it again before it *was* found. Well, Tom Tiddler, Gogmagog can only be got into the Leaden Hall by a trick. He's too strong to be forced, but you can always trick a giant, because Giants are as stupid as Goats.'

'Tcha-aah!' bleated Jerry, glaring with his yellow eyeballs at Simon.

'What's the matter? Sceptre in the throat?' hooted Simon, staring with his yellow eyeballs at Jerry. And Tom Tiddler noticed for the first time that though one was so wise, and the other so stupid, their eyes were of exactly the same colour. However, he couldn't stop to consider this just then, and he didn't want a quarrel, so he put his hand over Jerry's muzzle, and said, 'Please go on about the trick, Simon. Is it a hard one?'

'The best tricks are the simplest,' said Simon, 'and the simplest tricks are the oldest. This is a very old trick indeed. Now, Jinny Jones, did you say there was only one cherry-tree left in the Gardens with fruit on it?'

'Yes, please, Simon.'

'Then before Gogmagog wakes up, you and your friends must pick all the cherries off but one. Then you must bring them here and pass them through the gate to Tom Tiddler; but at each step on the way you must drop a cherry. After that, you must all go and hide behind the cherry-trees, and wait. That's all.'

'And what must *I* do?' asked Tom.

'I'll tell you, when you've got the cherries,' said Simon.

Off ran Jinny Jones with the little girls, and they did as they were told. They left just one big cherry hanging on the tree, and then stole back to the gate, dropping the cherries in a red line as they came. All the rest they pushed through the green lattice to Tom, and then they went and hid behind the trees.

And Simon told the end of the Trick in Tom's left ear.

30

THE LEADEN HALL

BEFORE LONG THERE was a great stir in the
Cherry Gardens. All the ground trembled. It was
Gogmagog stretching his limbs. Then all the leaves
began to blow about as though with a great wind. It was
Gogmagog drawing his waking-up breath. Then all the
sky filled with the sound of thunder. It was Gogmagog
yawning. Then a great crack seemed to cut across the
sound like a whip of lightning. It was Gogmagog
opening his eyes.

As soon as Gogmagog was well awake, he sat up and
roared:

'Jinny, bring me my breakfast, do!

If there aren't any Cherries, I'll eat you!'

All the little girls heard him, and trembled behind their
trees. Even Tom heard him, and shook his fist, though he
was now getting further and further away from the
Cherry Gardens, carrying out the end of the Trick.

When Jinny Jones didn't come, Gogmagog roared
again:

'I'll come to you, if you won't to me,

Where you're picking the very last cherry-tree!'

For Gogmagog knew that there was only one tree of cherries left in the Gardens, and that tomorrow he would have to have a little girl for breakfast instead. And he was rather cross about it, because he liked cherries best, and could never resist them, wherever they were.

When he reached the cherry-tree he was surprised to see no little girls there, and the tree stripped of its cherries. He was just about to ramp and rage through the Gardens in search of the children and the fruit, when his eye caught sight of the one cherry still hanging on the bough.

'I'll have that, anyhow!' said Gogmagog, and he picked and ate it. But he was used to eating cherries by the hundred at a time, and the tiny taste of one on his tongue only tantalised him.

So when his eye fell on the ground and saw another cherry under the tree, he said again, 'I'll have *that*, anyhow!' and stooped to pick it up; and while doing so he quite forgot about the little girls, because a Giant can only think one thought at a time, even if it's as tiny a thought as a cherry.

And dear me! no sooner had he stopped thinking of the second cherry, than he saw a third one a little way in front of him on the ground.

'I'll have *that*, anyhow!' said Gogmagog. And he ate the third cherry, and saw the fourth. So seeing, and saying, and stooping, and swallowing, he came in ninety-nine cherries to the Gate of the Cherry Gardens – and there, just outside it, lay the hundredth cherry!

'I'll have that, anyhow!' said Gogmagog, and he took the key of the Cherry Gardens from the chain round his neck, unlocked the Gate, and stepped outside.

In front of him lay a long line of cherries at even distances, so that as he swallowed each he had to take just *one* more step to get the next. And then he had to take just one more step, and just one more step, and just one more step, and just one more step. And at each step Gogmagog said, 'I'll have *that*, anyhow!' and he did not look to right or left, or to the rear. If he had, he would have seen all the little girls, led by Jinny Jones, creeping out of the gate behind him.

Through the streets stepped Gogmagog, and over a bridge, and through more streets again. But he saw nothing except the line of tempting cherries leading him through London step by step. At last the line stopped in front of a big dark Hall. The door of the Hall was open, and on the floor inside was a lighted candle, and round about the candle was, not one, but a whole heap of luscious red cherries.

'I'll have *those*, anyhow!' said Gogmagog. And he

stepped inside the Leaden Hall.

CLANG! crashed the door behind him.

Click! went the key in the lock.

'Hurray!' cried all the little girls, beginning to dance.

'Not so bad!' bleated Jerry, munching the last cherry-stalk Gogmagog had thrown down.

'Just an old trick they used to play in Greece,' hooted Simon, flying round and round the Leaden Hall.

And Tom ran up to Jinny and the little girls, crying: 'Oh, Jinny! Jinny Jones!'

'You can't catch *me*, Tom Tiddler!' laughed Jinny Jones, and ran away from him.

'Mary Brown! Betty Green!' then cried Tom Tiddler.

'You can't catch *us*!' laughed the little girls. And they *all* ran away from him.

31

Tom Tiddler's Ground

'OH, WELL,' SAID Tom.

He gathered up what was left of the cherries, just a basketful, and took them to Covent Garden.

All the stalls were there, full and ready, only the stall of the King's Cherry-Seller was as empty as usual, though the word

CHERRIES

was still written up over it in red and black letters as large as life.

As Tom entered the market on one side, a trumpet sounded on the other, and in marched the King's Cook followed by his Twelve Kitchen-Maids. He reached the front of the King's Cherry-Seller's stall just as Tom reached the back of it.

'What's the price of cherries today?' said the Cook.

'Sixpence a pound,' said the Cherry-Seller.

'I'll have ten pounds,' said the Cook.

'I haven't got ten pounds,' said the Cherry-Seller.

'Then I'll have all you've got,' said the Cook.

The Cherry-Seller said: 'I haven't got – and he was about to add 'any!' but just at that moment Tom thrust his basket of cherries on the counter from behind; so the Cherry-Seller swallowed his emotion very rapidly, and said, 'I haven't got . . . more than these.'

'Then I'll have those,' said the Cook. 'Weigh them!'

The Cherry-Seller weighed them, and they came to two pounds and three ounces.

'How much is that?' said the Cook.

'It's a shilling and something,' said the Cherry-Seller.

The Cook gave him a shilling and something (which turned out to be half a crown because he hadn't got a penny), and then the trumpet blew again, and the Cook bore away the cherries for King Lud's breakfast, followed by his Twelve Kitchen-Maids. All their faces were beaming with joy.

When the Courtiers saw the cherries on the breakfast-table they stopped shaking in their shoes at once, and King Lud's good-humour knew no bounds. He sent for the Cherry-Seller, and told him to name his own boon.

The Cherry-Seller said, 'So please your Majesty, can I have the Cherry Gardens for my own, because Gogmagog has left them for good and all? And so please your Majesty, can I set up an Inn there called the White

Heart, where people can come and drink Cherry Brandy and eat Brandy Cherries? And so please your Majesty, can I be made a Baron, and if I can, can I be called Baron Morella for ever and a day?'

'Certainly,' said King Lud, and he made him Baron Morella on the spot, and asked how it had come about that Gogmagog had left the Cherry Gardens. So the Cherry-Seller, who was a fair-minded man, told the King how it was really all Tom Tiddler's doings that he'd had cherries for breakfast, and King Lud turned to his Chamberlain and said,

'Isn't that the boy we put down on my Birthday Honours List?'

'Yes, Your Majesty,' said the Chamberlain.

'When *is* my Birthday?' asked the King.

'To-day, Your Majesty,' said the Chamberlain.

'How very fortunate,' said King Lud; and he had Tom Tiddler sent for, and told him to name his own boon. Then Tom asked, 'What is a boon?' and the King said, 'It's what you like.'

'Then, if you please, King Lud,' said Tom, 'I'd like you to let the Twelve Kitchen-Maids marry the Twelve Bakers, and I'd like the Head Baker to marry the Head Laundress.'

'They shall,' agreed King Lud.

'And please King Lud, I'd like you to let Wormwood

not have to scrub the slums any more, and I'd like you to let her have a new dress, so that she can go out with Arry every Bank Holiday.'

'She shan't. She shall,' agreed King Lud.

'And please King Lud, I would like the Shepherd and the Lavender Lass to live happy ever after.'

'They shall,' agreed King Lud.

'And please, King Lud, I would like you to set free the Moor, and let him go back to his own country.'

'Do you mean the Moor at the Gate?' asked the King.

'Yes, please, King Lud,' said Tom.

'But then we couldn't call it the Moor Gate any more,' said the King, beginning to look bothered.

'You could, your Majesty,' suggested Simon, 'if you planted heather there instead.'

The King looked much impressed, and said, 'What a good idea.'

'Yes,' agreed Jerry, 'heather is quite possible, at a pinch.'

So that was arranged. Then King Lud said,

'These aren't exactly the sort of boon I meant, for I don't see what good they do *you*, Tom Tiddler. So in addition, I hereby create you for ever and a day Master of the Streets of London Town, with all the Gold and Silver that is in them. And whoever comes picking of it up shall be accountable to you.'

'And may I go back to my own field for the holidays?' asked Tom.

'By all means,' said King Lud, 'if you won't miss the Gold and Silver too much.'

'Why, that's where all the Gold and Silver is!' said Tom Tiddler.

And that is nearly all. Only, whether he was in the Streets of London Town, or in his own Butter-cup-and-Daisy Field, Tom was always teased by the little girls who danced in and out and round about, trying to pick up his sixpences and his flowers before he could catch them.

'Here we come to Tom Tiddler's Ground!' sang Mary Brown.

'Picking up Gold and Silver!' sang Betty Green.

And Jinny Jones laughed, 'You can't catch *me*, Tom Tiddler! You can't catch *me*!'

And it was ever so many years before he did.

o' mine!' said the Chalk Farmer emphatically. 'It's weeks and weeks since I set eyes on 'em, the young rapscallions! There was none could quarry the chalk like Cliff, and none could burn it like Clem, but there! so soon as the work was done they must allus go a-birding, a-trying to lime the sparrows. Month afore last they slung a bag of the best lime over their shoulders, and went off after supper, having heard tell of a wondrous grove of birds somewheres or other that they were crazy to catch; and from that hour to this I've not seen a hair of their heads. And I took a vow that while they were gone nobody should lift a finger to do their work for 'em. That's why there's plenty of chalk, but no lime, brother.'

'Well, that's a pity,' said the Burly Baker, 'for it's like this here.' And he related to the Chalk Farmer how the Earl must have a White Chapel to be married in, and what would happen to Jinny Jones if he didn't. For Tom had confided the tale to him as they drove along.

The Chalk Farmer wagged his head and said: ''Tis a rare sad story, brother. Find me my two boys and bring 'em home, and you shall have lime enough to whiten St. Paul's, let alone a Chapel.'

'Don't you know where your boys went to, brother?'

'Nary a notion,' said the Chalk Farmer.

'Well, we'll be going,' said the Burly Baker, 'and see what we can do.'

'Have another snack first,' said the Chalk Farmer, flourishing his knife.

'No, no,' said the Burly Baker hastily, 'we must be off, thank you kindly, brother.' And he hurried out to his cart, bundling Tom and Jerry with him. The Chalk Farmer followed them to the door and watched them out of sight, still munching steadily at a lump of chalk.

'How *can* he?' asked Tom Tiddler, who hadn't been able to get down a crumb.

'Ah,' said the Burly Baker, 'my brother's one of them, you see, that can't tell chalk from cheese.'

19

THE MAIDEN IN THE LANE

'THE QUESTION IS,' said the Burly Baker as they drove along, 'which way?'

'Simon's good at answering questions,' said Tom. He tickled Simon under the wing, and asked, 'Which way, Simon?'

Simon ruffled his feathers a little and said huffily, 'Which way where?'

'To find out Clem and Cliff, the Chalk Farmer's sons.'

'You'll *never* find them out,' said Simon.

'Oh dear, oh dear!' said Tom, his mouth beginning to droop.

'But,' added Simon, 'you're *sure* to find them in.'

'In what?' asked Tom eagerly.

'In hiding,' said Simon.

'But why are they hiding?'

'Because they're wanted.'

'Who wants them?'

'You do, for one.'

'But they can't be hiding from me,' said Tom, 'because they don't know anything about me. You might tell, Simon.'

'Might is a big word,' said Simon, 'and covers a lot of ground. Your friend there' (and he cocked his head at the Burly Baker) 'might know better than to call me a fowl, as though I were a common Barndoor Hen. If you want to find out Clem and Cliff, you'd better ask the Maiden in the Lane. She has full instructions.'

'Ah, I know *her* right enough,' said the Burly Baker, 'and a spry little Maiden she is. As for calling you a fowl, bless me, you're that thick with flour there's no telling you from a hen or an eagle. But no offence meant.'

He flicked his whip, and trotted his horse smartly along till they reached the Maiden's Lane. The Maiden, a neat little figure in cap and apron, was walking down it eastward, carrying a loaded tea-tray very carefully.

'Hi! Maiden!' shouted the Baker, and pulled up his cart alongside.

The Maiden stopped and set down her tray. 'You shouldn't shout so sudden, sir,' she said reprovingly. 'Suppose I'd dropped the tea-things.'

'Not you,' said the Burly Baker: 'no one knows better than you where her hands and feet are.'

'Well, I will say I'm not a breaker,' said the Maiden. 'But I mustn't stand letting the tea get cold.'

'My Saturday Penny, ma'am?'

'Yes, to be sure. Old Ladies can't work for nothing, you know. I won't charge you more than a penny, because I know what little boys are, but if you've spent it already on marbles or jumbles, you must wait till next Saturday when your Daddy will give you another.'

'But, ma'am, I haven't a Daddy or a Penny,' said poor Tom, looking very crestfallen.

'Well, well, well, that's a case, to be sure. But I'll tell you what,' said the Old Lady comfortably, 'if you will fetch me a Spanish sword, that will do instead, for Spanish steel is very good steel, and makes capital needles.'

'But where shall I find a Spanish sword, ma'am?'

'Ah, I can't tell you *that*. If you find the means, I'll find the remedy. Till then, I'll put these tatters in with the rest of my mending.'

The Old Lady rolled up the lavender rags in a neat little bundle, and was about to drop them in the basket by her side when she saw that it had in it more than her mending. While she was talking, Jerry had leapt into the middle of the clothes, and was making hay of them with his horns. The Old Lady fished him out like a kitten, and held him up with his legs kicking in mid-air; but it was no use, the Old Lady's hands were as powerful as they were nimble.

'Jerry,' said the Old Lady, 'for I know you, to be sure!
– it's you and your like make all the trouble, and
trouble's the only thing you *do* make – everything else
you mar. But for you, I could sit now and then with my
hands in my lap, instead of always having to be mending
affairs with which you've played the giddy goat. Take
that!'

She gave him a great smack, and tossed him from her
with such force that he fell into the Stock-garden,
where he at once began to munch the flower-heads as
he lay. This brought the Bull down on him in double-
quick time.

'What are you doing here?' bellowed the Bull. 'Isn't
it enough to be pestered by a Bear, but I must be
plagued by a goat as well?'

Jerry lowered his horns, and the Bull lowered his;
and Jerry measured the Bull's horns by his own, and
thought better of it.

'If you please, sir,' said he, 'I'm not responsible for
myself.'

'Who is then?' asked the Bull.

Jerry jerked his head towards Tom, and said, 'Him!'

'Very well,' said the Bull, 'then I'll deal with both of
you at once. It's four o'clock, work's done for the day,
and I must shut up the Garden, and go home. Turn out!'

The Bear was already shuffling through the Garden

18

THE CHALK FARMER

THE BURLY BAKER'S cart rattled along at a fine pace, and Tom had too much ado to keep himself from being jolted out into the road to notice where they were going; but at last they pulled up before a comfortable farmhouse, white and lumpy, with a yellow thatched roof. It stood in a big round chalk quarry, and everything in sight was as thick with lime as it had been with flour in the Bakers' street. There were brown cows being milked by girls in pink frocks, and black pigs being fed by men in blue smocks; but they were all so dusty with chalk that the brown cows were the colour of whitey-brown paper, and the pink frocks like apple-blossom when it turns pale before falling, and the black pigs like mounds of grey cloud before sunrise, and the blue smocks like the summer sky seen through a morning mist. Lumps of chalk, big and little, littered the ground on all sides.

Beside the door was a wooden post with a big bell hanging from it. The Burly Baker pulled it, the

'Well, well,' said the Burly Baker, 'there's a way out of all trouble. Come Ralph, come George, heave the creature into that empty cart, and you, young sir, jump up alongside and take your fowl with you. I'll drive you myself to the Chalk Farmer, but if you can coax an ounce of lime out of him you'll be a smarter lad than I take you for. Once he has taken a vow, he'll break it for nobody, and I ought to know, for he's my own brother.'

the news of it travelled fast, and a big crowd of girls and boys gathered round to watch; and when the Head Baker stuck in the last almond, and stood back to consider the effect, a cheer of admiration broke from the children's throats. At the same moment the crowd parted, and a lovely little lady with a snow-white skin and shining, cream-coloured hair, came stepping in a white lace gown up the lane of boys and girls, as daintily as a little white pony in a circus. The Earl fell on his knee before her, and cried, 'Oh, my lady, is it white enough now?'

The little lady put her head first on one side and then on the other, looked the Chapel up and down and in and out, and answered,

'Yes, dear Earl, it is as white as lime itself, so send the invitation to the Spaniard, fetch the White Friar to marry us, lay the wedding-feast in the White Hall, and we'll be wedded by sundown.'

The Earl's face brightened with joy, for he saw the end of his waiting, and so did Tom's, for he saw the end of his wandering. The Bakers hastened away to prepare the feast, the Earl flew to write the invitations, and the Lady tripped home to put on her orange-blossoms. In two hours all was ready. The Earl's procession set out from his Court as the Lady's set out from her House. The Proud Spaniard walked beside the Earl, clanking his

17

THE WHITE CHAPEL

IT WAS A pretty little chapel, and had once been as white as a dove, but time had turned it to the colour of a London sparrow.

As soon as he set eyes on it, the Burly Baker said, 'Ah, that's a cake worth icing! Now, lads, fall to, and remember, careful does it!' So saying, he rolled up his sleeves, and the Twelve Bakers rolled up theirs.

Then what a stir and a bustle there was on all hands! Two bakers cracked the eggs and separated the whites from the yolks; two more whipped the whites to a standing foam, a third pair whipped the cream, the fourth pair sifted the flour, the fifth pair pounded the sugar to a powder, and the sixth pair blanched the almonds. Then, under the direction of their burly chief, the Twelve Bakers plastered the Chapel inside with flour, iced it outside with sugar, piled white of egg on the roof, coated the spire with cream, and when everything was done stuck it all over with almonds till it bristled like a hedgehog. While the work proceeded,

'Never heard of him, miss,' said the Burly Baker.

'In that case,' said the Maiden, 'Clement's in and Clifford's in. Step in, please.'

And in they stepped.

20

CLEMENT AND CLIFFORD

INSIDE THE ROOM sat two youths, fair and lanky, with pale faces. Between them on the table the tea-tray was set, but they had not yet begun to eat or drink. The Burly Baker clapped them on the shoulders, crying heartily, 'So there ye are at last!'

The two boys sprang up, put their fingers to their lips, and whispered, 'Hush! talk low, Uncle, talk low!'

'Bless me!' said the Burly Baker. 'What's the matter?'

'It's a matter of life and death,' said Clement.

'The Old Bailey's on our track,' said Clifford.

'What for?' asked the Burly Baker.

'Sit down and have tea,' said Clement, 'and we'll tell you. But who's this?' And he stared suspiciously at Tom.

'A young chap in trouble,' said the Burly Baker.

'Then he is one of us,' said Clifford, 'and as such he's welcome.'

They all sat down, and Clement cut the currant loaves into slices and buttered them thickly, while Clifford poured out the tea into the two cups